unexpected love story

NATASHA MADISON

Cover Design: Melissa Gill with MGBook Covers & Designs
Interior Design CP Smith
Editing done by Jenny Sims Editing for Indies
Proofing Julie Deaton Author Services by Julie Deaton

Dedication

Matteo, may you find someone who loves you
unconditionally, every step of the way.

Chapter One

Crystal

"Thank you so much for coming in." I smile at the receptionist while I hand her my insurance card. She looks at my name on the card, then gets up, and asks me to follow her.

"No problem," I reply, nodding at her. "I mean, I didn't think it was a suggestion when you called so ..." I remember the urgency in her voice when she called with my results and asked me to come in to the office.

"The doctor will be right in with you." She nods at me, then gestures for me to wait in his office. I look around at all the baby pictures lining his office walls. I smile at some of the red squished faces, thinking about if one of those was my child. Since I was five years old, the only thing I ever really wanted was to be a nurse and a mom.

I'm in my second year of John Hopkins University nursing school. However, the baby will have to wait just a bit or a while. I have my future semi-mapped out for me.

My first goal is to graduate nursing school at the top of my class. It's fucking on. My second goal is to be an emergency room nurse. The hustle and bustle are what I strive for, searching for the adrenaline rush. Making someone better, it is just … I sigh … amazing.

The doctor opens the door and enters. "Hey there, Crystal, thank you so much for coming in." The lack of eye contact worries me. Rule number one when you give bad news is not to make eye contact. My palms start to sweat as I sit here, wringing my hands. He pulls out his chair and sits in front of me, his eyes never meeting mine as he shuffles the papers on his lap.

My heart almost beats out of my chest, the sound echoing in my chest. I came in two weeks ago after not having had my period for six months. At first, I thought it was the stress of school and working. But then one month turned into two, and then there I was six months later.

"So we got your results back." Dr. Vincent starts talking as he lifts one paper over another. I look over to see if maybe I can see anything, but all the letters and numbers look like zeros.

"Is everything okay?" I ask, my voice trembling, my leg starting to shake on its own. I look down at my Converse, studying where the white part has turned a light gray from the dirt.

"I'm afraid it's not good." He closes the file and finally looks up to meet my eyes. Folding his hands on the file, I almost feel like he's protecting it. "The test results from the last time you came in are back. We conducted multiple tests."

"I know, I was there," I say. "I'm not dying, am I?" I laugh shakily, thinking this can't be fucking happening.

"No, no." He shakes his head. "You aren't dying."

I exhale and smile. "Well, that is good news, I think."

"It is, but there is bad news."

I chuckle. "I think me being able to live will outdo the bad news," I joke with him.

"You're sterile." Two words … two words I wasn't expecting to hear. Two words that make living not the best news. The tears come fast, they come hard, and my hand flies to my stomach as if to protect it.

"How can that be?" I shake my head, brushing the tears from my face. "It's not possible. There must be a mistake."

"I'm afraid I ran the test twice. That's why you haven't had your period. You don't ovulate."

"But I've gotten my period almost regularly since I was thirteen."

"It's almost as if your body is going through menopause."

"There must be something I can do. There must be something that can be done. I mean, I don't want to have a baby now, but eventually, I would like to become a mother." I'm trying to get him to tell me everything is going to be okay. I'm begging him to tell me I can have a baby.

He shakes his head. "I'm so sorry. I wish I could tell you that we can freeze some eggs. But the truth is that last time you came in, we checked and not one egg was released. You had none."

"What if I take hormones?" I sift through my medical knowledge in my mind but come up blank. "I'm nineteen. Are you saying I'm never going to be a mother? That my body is nineteen, but my uterus is fifty?" A sob breaks free.

"At this time, nothing you can take will help." He looks at me. "I wish there was something I could do."

"So what do I do?" I ask him, my chest heaving, my soul empty, and my heart broken. I will never hold my child in my arms. I will never have that moment when you sit down and feel your baby move inside you.

"There is always adoption," he tells me, but I shake my head.

"I think I just need to go." I get up from the chair and walk out of the office. My head is in a daze, and I keep my eyes downcast, not looking at anything but my feet. On the ride home, I feel like I'm on autopilot, just going through the motions.

Unlocking my apartment door, I'm happy my two roommates aren't home. Closing my bedroom door, I flip the lock. My jacket slides off my shoulders, and my shoes get kicked off. I fall onto my bed, bouncing as my body hits the mattress. I turn onto my side and gaze out the window. Little beads of water trickle down the glass. Was it raining? My hands go to my stomach, placing my palm on the emptiness that is inside. *Sterile.* One word with so many different meanings, but to me, it means one thing. My dreams are broken.

Crying into my pillow, I feel the sobs rip from my chest as I groan out my pain. The pain of never having my own child; the pain of never being able to give my husband a child.

My dreams are shattered, just like my heart. I sob until I have nothing left inside me and my heavy lids close. My phone rings somewhere in the distance. All my hopes and aspirations gone. "I'll never put someone else through this," I say to the empty room as my eyes fight to stay open. "I will never tell anyone," I whisper. "I will never." And my eyes close as my dreams are of darkness. Running. I'm always running. Running after my dreams. Running away from love. Running. Simply running.

Chapter Two

Crystal

Six Years Later . . .

"Two hours, people," I say to the people hustling in front of me. "Two more hours and I am off for four glorious days." I lean back in the chair, turning in a semi-circle. I am sitting at the nurses' station in the middle of the busiest emergency room in three counties.

"Four days off. I bet you get bored in about one day." Dawn, another ER nurse, laughs at me.

I turn to look at her. "Not this time. I have a date with my bed and my DVR."

She shakes her head as she continues to write on the chart in front of her. "How many patients do you have?" I ask her as I look over at the whiteboard that keeps track of the patients in the emergency room.

"I'm at twelve."

"You want me to take two? I only have eight." I look

over at the board, wondering if any would give me a challenge. We are a busy ER, but nothing urgent has been brought in. The phone on the counter rings.

It is the phone that the dispatch calls when an ambulance is on its way in. "Dibs." Dawn does not even bother to look up when I jump up.

"Crystal speaking." It's routine to just give my name.

"Hey, Crystal." I hear Carole's voice on the line. "We have an ambulance coming in Code one, R-twenty-three. Status zero. ETA is three minutes." Her voice goes quiet.

"Fuck." I hang up the phone. "We have an accident victim coming in, and he's DOA." I walk around the desk and jog to the back where the ambulances come in. Holding my stethoscope, I look down at my black Crocs, taking in the outside sun. I haven't been outside today, but it looks like it's clear without a cloud in the sky. I spot the white ambulance backing in, and Dr. Arnold appears next to me. "I hate these calls," I tell him.

Dr. Arnold and I started here at the same time. He's the only doctor I actually like working with, and that's only because he lets me do my thing. He lets me treat the patient and asks my opinion. "Hey, who knows. Maybe we can be this man's miracle today."

I shrug my shoulders, jogging outside with him as the EMTs pull the gurney out. "What do we have, boys?"

"We have a twenty-eight-year-old male, hit by a truck with an impact of ___ miles per hour. He was down when we arrived and initiated three rounds of CPR, shocked him twice, and injected a half milligram of epi through his IV. We intubated him on scene with ten liters per minute O2 at respirations of ten breaths per minute. Blood pressure is eighty palp, pulse forty-eight weak and irregular. No immediate changes and transported emergent," one of the guys says as I look down at the patient. My heart stops or rather speeds up.

"Eric," I whisper, and everyone stops moving, looking back at me. "It can't be. What is the victim's name?" I look at the two EMTs, waiting for their answer. Waiting for them to tell me it's all a mistake.

"Eric McIntyre Schneider," Chad, one of the EMTs, tells me.

"Fuck." I turn to Dr. Arnold. "This is Hailey's husband." He just nods at me.

"Let's try to make a miracle happen." I nod, and we start running with the gurney. "What are his vitals, or what were his vitals?"

"He was DOA. We did CPR for three minutes but nothing. We shocked him twice and nothing."

We make it to ER room five. "Firemen had to saw him out of the car."

"On my count," Dr. Arnold says, telling us we are transferring him from the gurney to a hospital bed in three seconds. "One, two, three." We move him to the bed. I take out my scissors, cutting through his t-shirt, careful of the shards of glass falling off him. Not a speck of blood is present, but you can tell his chest has been crushed. I look at his face and see the swelling starting. His cheek appears shattered. Pale bruises forming where the blood has stopped flowing lead me to guess it's been about thirty minutes since his heart has stopped. Thirty minutes without oxygen to his brain, which means he wouldn't survive no matter what we did. No matter how long we worked on him, he was gone. His fingernails are white, but his hands are tinged blue. I look up at Dr. Arnold, who looks at me with a defeated look.

"I'm sorry," he whispers as the EMT techs just look down.

"He was T-boned by an eighteen wheeler," the EMT says, trying to make me see nothing could have been done. Nothing anyone could have done. He was gone.

Dealing with death is just a part of this job you have to come to terms with. Normally, I can block it out, but I can't do it this time. "Time of death, twelve thirteen," Dr. Arnold says, looking at the clock on the wall over the door.

I nod and walk out of the room, the tears burning my eyes while my heart starts to beat so fast, my breathing starts to block in my chest. I lean with my hands on my knees, the sting of breathing hurting. "I will handle it," Dr. Arnold says, letting me know he would inform my family.

I stand, praying for the strength. "I got it," I tell him, going over to the nurses' station. I sit in the chair I was just in moments ago and pick up my cell phone to call Blake.

"Hey," he answers, chipper.

"There was an accident." My voice doesn't raise; it doesn't go lower. It stays monotone. "Eric."

"Where is he?" Blake asks right away. I hear what sounds like running, then a car door slamming. I think it sounds like tires screeching, but I'm not even sure at the moment.

"He was DOA," I finally say out loud, my body slumping in the chair. "There was nothing we could do." I don't even bother finishing because Blake is talking now.

"Call Hailey and tell her I'm on my way. I'm four minutes out." He disconnects, and I feel a hand on my shoulder. Looking up, I see it's Dawn.

"Do you want me to take over?" she asks. The news has already spread in the ER.

I shake my head as a tear slips out of my eye. I pick up the phone to call Hailey, gazing at the picture of us smiling at the camera. She is my best friend. But more importantly, she's my cousin. She is my person. She is the one I would die for, the one who I know would die for me. I would use my one phone call on her, but knowing us, she would probably be with me. Growing up, I was older by six months, and she never let me forget it.

The phone rings three times before she picks up, and I hear the song "Glorious" in the background. "Hello," she answers almost breathlessly.

"It's me." I try to mask my voice, but I'm not sure I'm doing a good job. "Where are you?" My voice tries to stay calm, tries to stay monotone, but toward the end, it cracks, and she knows I'm not okay. That nothing is okay.

"I'm home," she whispers into the phone. I gather the strength I need to get through the phone call—one more minute before I can break down without her hearing it.

"You need to come to the hospital." I keep the sob at bay, impeding the trembling of my voice. "Blake is on his way to get you." I think of her at her house; the house she shares with Eric, her husband of six months. I think of the fact she will go back there alone tonight. Tears roll down my cheeks, and my nose starts to run. I grab a Kleenex and bring it to my face. "You need to get in the car, okay?" I say softly but firmly. "Listen to me, Hailey. Go outside and get here." She doesn't say anything as the call is disconnected, and I know Blake got there. The phone slips from my hand as I get up, rounding the nurses' station as my aunt and uncle come running through the door. One look at them, and I let go of my pain. My uncle grabs me in his arms as I sob on his shoulder. "He's gone." Two words. Why does everything bad only take two words? Two fucking words break me for the second time in my life.

I have my breakdown while my aunt rubs my back. "I need to go clean my face. Hailey will be here in a couple of minutes, and I have to be strong for her." He just looks at me. "Dawn." I look at the desk and find it's not just Dawn, but also Cori, Melanie, and Marie all standing there. My work wives all ready to hold me up.

"We can do this," Cori says as they all nod next to her.

"I need to wash my face." I turn, walking into the bathroom, and splash my face with cold water. I look at my face; the redness of my eyes evident. "You can do this," I tell my reflection. "You have to do this." I do what I do best—close myself off, remove myself. Except no matter how much training I've had, nothing could have prepared me for what is to come. Nothing.

I come out of the bathroom and go to the nurses' station. Sitting here, I look at the clock. The ticking from the second hand echoes loudly in the room full of hustle and bustle. The nurses are still working. Patients are still coming in. It's almost as if I'm watching this from out of my body. My eyes try to focus on the movement of my aunt when she finally sees Hailey walk in. Her eyes scanning everywhere as she looks for answers. Her face pale, drained from the happiness there just this morning when she was gushing about Eric being back after being gone a month. She looks up at Blake, asking him questions while she walks down the hallway. I walk around the desk, and her eyes find mine.

She stops in her tracks. I look at her, my brain telling me to remain focused, but my heart takes over as I try to calm my trembling lower lip. She tries to walk forward, but instead, she falls to her knees. When her blood-curdling wail fills the room, I rush to her. She turns her head, not aware the sound is coming from her.

She is on her hands and knees in the middle of the hospital corridor. Her eyes find mine, and her screaming stops. I don't think she realizes she is the one screaming because she has detached from her body. But by the look she gives me, I know she knows. A look of helplessness overtakes her. She knows nothing will ever be the same again. Her eyes close as I hold her in my arms as she turns her face to me and her tears soak through my blue scrubs.

Chapter Three

Crystal

I rock her from side to side until Blake approaches us. He picks her up as I peel her off my chest. She doesn't even stir; he carries her to the dreaded fucking white room. The room of death as we all call it. He places Hailey on a chair as my uncle cradles her in his arms.

I get up, and Blake pulls me to the side. "What the fuck happened?"

"It was a head-on collision," I say with a low voice, hoping no one else hears me. "He was DOA." I'm about to tell him something else when I hear Hailey's broken voice.

"Where is he?" She tries to stand, her legs still weak. My uncle turns to her, trying to talk her out of it, but she snaps.

"I need to see him." I know from her tone that it isn't a request. She's demanding to see him with her own eyes; she needs to see this isn't just a dream. She looks up at me, and I know nothing will change her mind. I hold my hand out to her, trying to give her my strength. I try to give her whatever she needs from me in order to get through this.

"I have to warn you ..." I try to find the words to tell her that it isn't him. He doesn't even look like himself anymore. I don't have a chance to tell her anything else because, at that moment, two officers walk into the waiting room. They look around, and once their eyes fall on me, they freeze. One of the officers is Frank Vincent, and we went to high school together. His face says it all as he tries not to make eye contact with Hailey. He comes forward, taking off his hat, carrying a plain brown bag in his hand. It looks like the bags we hand over to the family members when the patient is no longer with us. The only things left of that person is in one fucking bag. I don't even hear what Frank tells her because my eyes focus on the brown fucking bag.

She nods at him, while he hands holds the bag while her eyes stay focused on it. I drag her away from everyone, walking us into another room, and close the door behind me. Her eyes never fucking leaving that bag that she holds in her hands.

"Listen, Hailey. I know you want to see him, I do. I know. But I'm going to be very honest with you. You won't recognize him." I stop talking to take a deep breath and push down my sorrow and sadness. "I promise you that if I thought seeing him would help you, I would bring you to him right now, but it's not Eric. It's not your husband." I can't stop the tears that slip out. I

14

can't stop the look of pain she gives me, either. Tortured. Broken. Empty.

"This is a dream, right?" Tears fall down her face again, making new tracks. "This isn't happening to me. It's not him, right? It's just a terrible misunderstanding. That's the only way any of this would make any sense." She almost begs me to tell her it isn't him. And at that moment, I want to. I want to go back there and pound on his chest until his heart starts beating again. At that moment, I know miracles don't fucking happen.

"I'm so sorry, honey. It's him. I wish I could take your pain away. I would do anything to take it away." I walk to her and wrap my arms around her. My hand meets her cold body; it's almost as if she is standing in the middle of a snowstorm without a jacket. Her sobs start quietly, but before long, the wails fill the room. And as she slowly goes limp in my arms, I hold her body as much as I can till we are both on the floor, her body lying in my lap, as I take in her closed eyes.

"Blake!" I scream. The door is opened, and he rushes in. "Get Dawn." He turns to run away as I lift her arm, taking her pulse. It's elevated, but I wouldn't expect anything less.

Dawn rushes in the room with Dr. Arnold right behind her. "I think she fainted, I caught her before she hit her head,"

I tell them as Dr. Arnold takes her vitals and checks her.

"She's in shock. What do you want to do?" He looks at me. "We can keep her here, or you can take her home."

"Home," Blake and I both say. "The last thing she needs is to be in a room two feet away from her dead husband," I whisper to him, and he nods his head.

Blake walks over and picks her up in his arms for the second time today. "Help me put her in my truck," he tells me as my uncle holds up my aunt, who is quietly sobbing in his arms. I follow Blake out to his truck, opening the door so he can place Hailey in the seat. The brown fucking bag clutched in her hands so tightly, her fingertips are white. Nothing will take that bag away from her. Nothing will let her drop it.

The sun heats my face as I stand here watching him buckle her in. After closing the door, he says, "Get in." I just nod at him, open the back door, climb in, and fasten my seat belt. As I look out the window, I grab my phone that I had in the back of my scrub pants and text Dawn. It's the only thing I took when I walked out with Hailey.

I'm on my way to Hailey's.

She texts me back right away.

We got you covered. Don't worry about us. Let me know if you need anything.

I smile and put my phone away. I need fucking tequila or whiskey. We pull up to Hailey's house before I even have a chance to decide. I jump out of the truck, opening the passenger door to unbuckle her, and help her get out.

I follow Blake and Hailey as they walk up the step to her house, their house. The house where Eric and Hailey lived.

I walk in and take in the house. You know right away Eric is home. As an aircraft engineer, he was always on the road, but when he was home, his things were all over the house. A tossed sweater here; an empty mug by the couch. And now is no different. His sweater is tossed over the couch. Hailey walks over to the mug left beside the couch and picks it up.

"He just got home last night," she whispers at us, looking up. "Maybe if he didn't come back, he would still be here. Maybe," she trails off in a whisper. I look at Blake, telling him silently to get rid of anything that shouldn't be out of place. He knows what I mean by just a look, walking to the kitchen, and I turn to walk toward Hailey.

"Why don't I take you upstairs and you can lie down for a bit?" I ask. She sets the mug and brown paper bag down, walking toward the stairs.

"Don't touch his things," she tells me, looking over her shoulder. I follow her as she walks in their bedroom. The bed still fucking unmade. His work pants over a chair in the corner. His work boots right next to them. Exactly where he took them off. His bathrobe is lying across the end of the bed. She walks over to it, picking it up and wrapping it around her. She falls onto the bed and curls herself into the fetal position. Blocking herself from the hurt, she's preventing anything else from getting in.

I watch her from the doorway till her breathing evens out. When I hear the front door open, I turn to walk down the steps and come face to face with my aunt Joanne. Her eyes red still.

"Where is she?" she asks, taking off her jacket and tossing it on the couch right next to Eric's sweater.

"She is sleeping or resting," I answer her quietly. "I don't even know anymore." I walk into the kitchen and head to the cabinet that holds the whiskey. I take out the bottle and set it on the counter. My aunt places the brown fucking bag on the counter next to the bottle, putting the mug in the sink.

I reach out to grab a glass to pour a shot in. I shoot it back, the burn going from my lips, all the way down my throat, and hitting my stomach. It warms right through me. I look back to see Blake leaning against the counter. "You want one?" I ask. He just nods, so I pour him the same amount in the same glass and hand it to him. He tosses it back without wincing like I did.

"How the fuck did this happen?" I ask the room, and no one answers me. No one even looks up. I pour another shot and immediately down it. This time with less burn. "I'm going to go lie with her in case she wakes up in a panic."

Blake nods, so I walk out of the room and make my way upstairs. She hasn't moved since I left; her breathing is still the same except you can hear little hiccupping sobs between breaths. I can only imagine her dreams.

I lie next to her, my eyes finding the window as I watch the sky turn from blue to black. I know right away when she is awake; her breathing isn't the same, it's not smooth. She's taking deep, deep breaths now.

"Is it real?" she asks, knowing I would be here, knowing that she would be here for me. She doesn't wait for me to answer.

"My chest hurts. My heart hurts," she whispers the last part, and I turn to put my arms around her as tears stream down both of our faces. "Did he suffer?"

It's a question that everyone asks. "No," I answer as my voice cracks and a sob tries to come out. "He was already gone when they brought him in."

"Do you think he knew today was going to be his last day?" Her questions gut me; questions I have no answers for. That no one can answer. "Do you think he knew? What am I supposed to do now?" She turns and looks at me. She searches my eyes for the answers, but I don't have them. Her eyes close again as if she is chasing the good dreams.

"Do you want something to eat?" I ask her, knowing full well she isn't going to eat anything. Her hand goes to her chest, and she tries to rub away the pain. "You need to at least drink something." I get up off the bed and look over at her, giving her a moment to … I don't even know what; there is nothing for her to wrap her mind around. Her husband is dead; half her soul is gone. I walk downstairs; looking in the kitchen, I find Blake is now sitting at the kitchen table with my aunt. "She's up," I tell them both as I look over at the empty whiskey bottle. "You couldn't even save me a shot?" I look over at Blake, recognizing the emptiness in his eyes.

"I should make her something to eat," my aunt Joanne says, and I scoff. "She needs to eat even if it's just a bite." She gets up, going to the fridge.

I nod, opening the cupboard to grab a glass to pour water into and then walk over to the coffeemaker and pour a cup of coffee.

"I'm going to go get her," I tell them, walking back upstairs with the coffee and water. I've given her enough time by herself. "Your mom wants to make you something to eat even if it's just toast."

"I'm not hungry." She turns, burying her face in Eric's pillow. "He's really gone?"

Wiping away a tear falling down my face, I walk to her and sit down on the side of the bed. "We will get through this. I promise you." I wish I had more conviction. I wish I believed the words myself. I wish I knew how.

"I don't think I will ever get over this." She closes her eyes again, getting lost in her memories. Getting lost in the happy dreams, instead of staying here in the darkness, where there are no answers and where there is nothing but pain.

Chapter Four

Gabe

"I can't believe that in forty-five minutes, you're going to be a married man," my cousin Walker says from beside me on the couch. I look up at him, taking in our tuxes.

"I can't fucking wait," I tell him while my other cousin Brody comes into the room. "I will also say I'm never planning another fucking wedding again in my life." I bring the glass of scotch to my lips.

Ever since I proposed to Bethany, my life has been turned upside down. Bethany and I met when we were both in college. My father and I run the best medical clinic in five counties. My father was old school, but when I came in, I brought new technology with me. In the five years I've been with him, we have grown tenfold. Out are the old machines, and in are the state-of-the-art machines. It was a gamble we decided to take, and it's paid off so much. We are even looking at expanding and adding a pediatric wing.

I fell in love with her the minute I saw her, her blond hair perfect, her body even better. She was a debutant, a true Southern woman. I asked her out after a month, and we have been together ever since.

Standing in the middle of the vacant lot I just bought for us to build our dream home on, I proposed. I got down on one knee and promised her the moon and stars. She accepted and then my life went into overload. Between work and the planning of this circus that is now my wedding.

I didn't give a shit where we did it or who was there, but her parents took over, and it rose to five hundred invites. In the meantime, she was building us a castle. Or at least that was what I thought. Every suggestion I had was thrown out the window, but I didn't give a shit. I just wanted her to be happy.

"Jesus, I don't think I've seen that many people in my life." Brody walks in, pulling the collar of his tux away from his neck. "This fucking monkey suit is strangling me."

Walker laughs at him as he throws himself down in the chair next to him. "The good news is that the house is finally finished and everything moved in. You get to sleep in your bed tonight." He lifts his glass to me.

"Finally," I say, thinking about how we've been living in Bethany's little apartment while we wait for the house to be built.

The knock on the door makes me look up, and I see Mila, Walker's four-year-old daughter, bounce in. "Poppa." She comes in wearing the white flower girl dress. "I got a basket of flowers." She tries to climb on the couch, but the puffy dress makes it almost impossible. My gram walks in next, dressed in a brown gown.

"Are you boys ready?" she asks, looking around at us. "Jensen, don't give him too much to drink." My cousin's name is Jensen Walker, but the only one to actually call him Jensen is my gram.

Walker's father and my father are brothers. Walker's father passed away the year after he retired, leaving Walker to take over Walker Construction. Like me, he brought in new things, and his company blew up. He married his high school sweetheart, but she left him with a Dear John letter two weeks after his daughter was born.

Left him and their daughter for his best friend. It's been four years, and I still haven't seen him on a date. I smile at his beautiful daughter, hoping that Bethany gets pregnant right away. We discussed it, and we both want big families.

"Okay, boys." I down the rest of my scotch. "Let's go get me married." I clap my hand, putting on the jacket to my tux and pulling down the cuffs. Gram takes Mila by the hand and walks out of the room.

"All for one," Brody starts, and Walker and I both finish, "one for all." It was our motto growing up. The three of us never strayed far from the others. The three amigos they called us, but we always corrected them with the three musketeers. We thought it sounded manlier.

We walk out of the back of the church and into the side door. I take in the flowers all over the church. The smell of roses hits me right away when I walk in. I step up to the altar, taking in the church. It's packed to the gill and down to standing room only. I nod at a couple of people who I recognize on my side of the church. My parents sit in the front row, a smile on their face as they watch their only child get married. My father puts his arm around my mother's shoulders, bringing her in and kissing her forehead.

From as far back as I can remember, my parents have never shied away from affection. That and they love each other with everything they have. I want that. And I finally found it with Bethany.

I smile as the music starts. Her parents walk down together, and I silently nod at them. Bethany was adamant about walking down the aisle by herself. "I'm an independent woman, Gabe," she would always say.

Next up is Bethany's sister, who smiles the whole way. Then little Mila walks down the aisle, stealing the show. I look over to see Walker with the biggest smile on his face and nothing but love for her.

She goes to sit with Walker's mother. "I did it, Grandma," she yells and has everyone chuckling.

Bethany's best friend, Amilia, walks down next. The doors of the church close behind her as she marches down the aisle. I stand here with my hands crossed in front of me when the "Wedding March" begins to play. Everyone rises to their feet in anticipation of the bride coming down the aisle.

I hold my breath, looking down and then up again, but the doors remain closed. I look over at Amilia, who just shrugs. The song finishes, and the doors stay closed. I look over at Walker and Brody, who both have a worried look on their faces. I am about to walk to the back of the church to see if she is okay when the doors finally open. I breathe a sigh of relief, but it is short lived when I look up and see the wedding planner, Jennifer, walking down the aisle. She keeps her head down as she makes her way to the altar. My heart rate picks up as the heat on my neck rises, and I suddenly feel like the shirt is suffocating me.

Jennifer walks up the four steps to approach the altar. "Gabe," she whispers, coming close to me.

"Is everything okay?" My palms start to sweat. "Where is she?"

She glances down at her feet, then looks up at me with tears in her eyes. Looking over my shoulder at Walker, she softly says, "She isn't coming."

"What do you mean she isn't coming?" My voice rises a bit. Walker approaches one side of me, and Brody walks to the other side.

"She got here with everyone, and she waited till Amilia walked down the aisle. She handed me this and then took off in a cab parked on the side of the church." She hands me a white note.

"I don't understand." I snatch the white paper from her, unfolding it and seeing Bethany's handwriting.

Gabe,

I can't do this. I can't go through with this. I made a horrible, horrible mistake by accepting your proposal.

It was what was expected of me, but I can't go

through with it. I've taken a job in Chicago. I'm so, so sorry that I didn't have the courage to tell you to your face.

Bethany

"Oh my god." I hear Walker next to me, but my eyes never leave the paper. I never look up from her note. Bethany's mother walks up to see me, grabbing the paper from me.

"She fucking left me." I turn, looking at Walker and then Brody, who is now joined by Darla at his side. "She left me at the fucking altar." I throw my head back and laugh, hysterically. I'm having a stroke; that must be the reason. I turn to look at the whole church as the whispering starts. I look at my parents, my mother dabbing away her tears while my father whispers in her ear.

"Well, folks …" I say loudly, laughing instead of crying.

I hear Amilia say, "He's losing his mind."

I turn to her. "Might be just that. We have a runaway bride," I announce. Some gasp in shock, and others look anywhere except for at me. "Please feel free to attend the reception as the Hickmores have already paid for everything." I nod then turn around. "Someone get me the fuck out of here," I say, ripping the top button off my tux. Walker and Brody both nod at me.

"You take him," Darla says. "I'll handle all this."

Walker nods at her as Brody leans down to kiss her. "Thanks, babe," he says as we walk out the side door we entered earlier. "We need a fucking ride," Brody starts.

"You just swore in church," I point out to him.

Brody shakes his head and smiles, "Dude, I can safely say I wasn't the only one swearing in that church in the past five minutes. I'm sure the Hickmores said fuck when you invited everyone to stay for the reception."

Seeing the limo that probably brought Bethany here. "You." I point at the limo driver. "I'll pay you double to get me the fuck out of here." He nods his head as we all climb into the backseat. Brody reaches for the champagne, but I snatch it from him and toss it out the door. "Fuck that shit," I say, and no one says a word. I lean my head back, the pounding becoming increasingly louder and louder. "I am never fucking getting married," I say to the quiet of the car. "I need to get so shitfaced I don't remember today." I look out the window, thinking how fast my perfect day turned into a day of fucking hell.

Chapter Five

Crystal

"I don't think she is going to eat any of this," I say, looking around the kitchen at the fried chicken my aunt just made.

"She needs to eat," Blake says from his chair. I turn to glare at him.

"I'm aware, but she just lost her husband and probably feels dead inside. You really think she is going to come down and eat fried chicken?" He doesn't answer; instead, he looks down at the empty whiskey glass he's spinning on the table.

"We have to make the arrangements," I say, rubbing my forehead. "What a fucking clusterfuck. I can't even imagine what she's feeling right now."

Blake opens a new bottle and pours himself another shot, swallowing it down, and I look at him. "I'm so sorry. I shouldn't …" I remember when he had to bury his first love when cancer took her at nineteen. He has never been the same.

I don't say anything to him because I hear the creaking of the stairs. Looking down the hallway, I see Hailey coming downstairs. Her hair tied on top of her head, the robe is still wrapped around her. Her eyes are swollen from the tears she has shed the whole day.

"Hey," I whisper to her, "you hungry?" I ask her but she doesn't even acknowledge me. She looks around the room at the table set, but as soon as her eyes land on the brown bag on the counter she is in a trance. She turns on her feet, heading straight to the brown bag. My eyes find Blake's, and we both inhale deep.

The crinkling of the bag fills the silence of the room as the four of us stand, waiting for her to fall. Waiting to catch her.

Opening the bag, she takes out his watch first. When she looks at it, the sob rips out of her. She brings the watch to her nose and smells it, her other hand gripping the counter to hold on to it. I step forward but stop when she sets it down. I don't see what she pulls out next because the tears block my vision.

"This isn't his." She turns to us, holding a black iPhone. "His phone was white."

I walk over to her, this time to help her stand. "Maybe it was put in there by mistake. Here, let me plug it in, and we can see who the phone belongs to." I grab it from her and walk over to the wall charger, plugging it in. The red dead battery sign lights up.

I look back at her as she runs her fingers over his phone, her eyes closing as tears drip off her chin, almost like you left the faucet on. "We took this picture last week after he got home. He was gone for a month this time. It was the longest he'd ever been away." She looks up at us, the hollowness almost too much to bear. "How did this happen?" She looks at each of us separately as she waits for an answer. My aunt and I are brushing our own tears off our face when the buzzing on the counter starts.

Hailey walks over to the phone before I can get to it and presses the button. Her face goes white, whiter than it was, her lips almost turning ash. Her hands start shaking, shaking so much the phone slips out of her hand and lands right in front of her feet.

The phone faces all of us, and I finally see what shocked her. The picture on the screen is Eric with another woman and kids. I don't have time to let it sink in, I don't have time to comprehend what this means, because the phone is now ringing with the word *Baby* on it.

The room stands here in shock, my aunt's hand going to her mouth. My arms hang by my sides, heavy, so heavy I can't reach out and grab the phone from Hailey before she bends down and presses the green button.

My heart is breaking, my inner voice yelling *No*. My breathing comes in spurts, almost as if I've just run a marathon. I don't hear her voice when she answers because the whooshing of my heart fills my ears.

The four of us are rooted to the spot. The phone finally slips out of her hand, and we all spring into action. Blake rushes to grab Hailey before she falls, the phone stopping right in front of my feet. "Hello?" I hear being shouted from the phone. "Hello?" I finally bend down and pick up the phone, bringing it to my ear.

"Hello." I finally find the words that have been lodged in my throat.

"Who is this?" whispers the female voice.

"This is Crystal," I finally say, turning and walking out of the room. Stepping out the front door, I sit on the first step. "Who is this?"

"Samantha." Her voice cracks. "Who are you guys, and why do you have Eric's phone?" I can't see her face, but from her voice, I can tell she's just as terrified and broken as we are.

"Are you …?" I don't even know what to ask. "Who are you to Eric?"

"I'm his wife." My eyes close as I take in the implication of what she just said about that motherfucking bastard. "And I'm tired of answering questions without getting any answers of my own."

"I," I start, saying slowly, "where are you?"

"I'm at home," she answers right away.

"I need you to sit down," I tell her, knowing I am going to have to break the news to her that her scumbag husband is dead. "There has been an accident."

"Oh my god," she whispers, and I hear her sobbing right away. The screen door opens, and I feel Blake sit next to me. I put her on speakerphone.

"Is he okay?" she asks between sobs. I shed one single tear for this woman, and Blake takes the phone from me.

"He didn't make it," he says curtly, not even sugarcoating anything as the wails come through the phone. We hear a little girl's voice in the background. "Mommy, Mommy, are you okay, Mommy?" And now I can't stop the tears.

"Where …" She starts breathing heavily. "Where is he?"

"He's at Mercy General hospital," Blake says. "I'm sorry for your loss, but I have to know … who are you?"

"I'm his wife," she says as Blake's hand tightens around the phone, his knuckles going white. "We've been married for twelve years. We have two girls." Her voice fades, and we hear shouting in the background.

"What the fuck is going on?" a male voice shouts. He must grab the phone from Samantha because now he's on the phone. "Who the fuck is this?" His voice is almost identical to Eric's.

"Where is Samantha?" Blake asks right away, his protector going to work.

"She's right next to me. Now answer my fucking question."

"There was an accident today. Eric didn't make it."

"Fuck," the voice on the other end hisses. "Where is he, and who is this?"

"He's at Mercy General Hospital. My name is Blake. He was married to my sister."

"That's impossible," the man's voice whispers urgently. "He's already married to Samantha."

"Yeah," Blake says, nodding his head. I lean my head on his shoulder, thinking that this just got more fucking fucked up than before. Now not only do we have to mourn Hailey's husband, but we also have to come to terms with the fucker's double life.

I didn't think she would be able to survive losing him, but I know this last piece of information will fucking break her. I look straight ahead, not paying attention to the rest of Blake's conversation. I close my eyes, my body almost numb.

He hangs up the phone and places it next to him gently, the phone already shattered from when it slipped out of Hailey's hand. "I don't even want to know how she is going to survive this. I can't do it," I say softly. "I can't tell her. I just …" A sob finally breaks free, and I put my hand on my mouth to block the sound. Blake wraps his arm around my shoulders, bringing me even closer as I bury my face in his shoulder. My tears seeping into his shirt.

Giving me the time to purge it from my system, he doesn't say anything while I let my pain go. "You good?" he asks when I stop crying, and I just nod my head. "We need to go inside and let them know." He gets up, holding his hand out to me. "Just let me do all the talking."

"I wouldn't be able to even if I wanted to," I tell him as we walk inside and break the news to them that Eric—sweet, caring Eric—was, in fact, a two-timing asshole with a wife and family.

I sit down with my eyes on my hands. My mind blanks as I watch Hailey's face while we tell her that her husband isn't her husband but someone else's. I sit here watching her as this information sinks in. I sit here empty and hollow with nothing left to give.

Cursing him in my head, I sit here wishing him all the pain in the world. I sit here wishing he was still alive—not for Hailey, but so I could inflict pain on him. I wish he was here, so he could face what he left behind. I wish … at the end of the day, we all have different wishes. I stop my thoughts when I hear Hailey yell, grabbing the picture of her and Eric from beside her and hugging it to her chest.

The doorbell makes us all look up, and if I thought it was bad before, well, let's just say that we all went down that fucking rabbit hole.

Chapter Six

Gabe

"Is that banging?" I ask as my head comes off the couch, my tongue thick. "What is that?" I ask, looking around. *Where the fuck am I?* Looking down, I see I'm still wearing my wrinkled tux pants and white shirt.

And it all comes back to me. I was left at the altar. Coming to the home we didn't even live in yet. Having only moved our stuff in, we were waiting for the wedding night to officially move in. I went to the kitchen and pulled out all the booze, all the fucking booze, and guzzled it down to stop the pain in my chest. I look over to see Walker walking into the room with coffee in his hand and Advil in the other. "You need to sober up just a bit." He set the cup on the coffee table tray. "We need to do a couple of things."

"I'm pretty sure me getting stood up at the altar wasn't on the list of things to do, yet I did it." I try to make a joke of it before I drink the scalding coffee, which burns all the way down my throat. "What the fuck could we possibly need to do?"

"We need to pack up Bethany's things." He looks over at me.

"Fuck that. I say we have a bonfire on the beach and burn all her shit." I smile, thinking that the fire would probably be out of control for all the shit she has here. "Scratch that." I shake my head, the pounding making me wince. I walk into the kitchen, open a drawer, and take out a pair of scissors. "Grab some boxes from the garage."

I walk to the winding steps in the middle of the house, taking them two at a time on the way to our bedroom. I walk into our huge master bedroom with wooden beams across the ceiling.

Passing the king-size bed in the middle of the room, I head to her walk-in closet. It's the size of an office, but I couldn't say no to her. Her clothes are all hung by color; I guess she was planning a wardrobe change as well since everything looks to be here. Meaning she took fucking nothing with her. I rip piece by piece down, cutting each one right down the middle and then throwing it on the floor. The whole time, Walker leans against the doorjamb, letting me do my thing. I get to the pants, cutting off a leg from each of them. "Good luck trying to get that back in one piece." I laugh at myself. I cut the skirts in half. "That isn't going to be good to wear." I look over at Walker, who just shakes his head. I pick up the shoes— oh, her perfect shoe collection. "Do you know she made me pay four thousand dollars for a pair of shoes for the wedding? Four fucking thousand dollars!"

I pick up a dainty pair of shoes with the red bottoms and snap off the heel. "That's not going to work." I go all through her shoe collection. "I must have spent twenty grand on shoes." I look down at the dismantled shoes. "What the fuck was I thinking?"

"You just wanted to make her happy." Walker finally speaks.

"A lot of good that did me." I look around. "I'm stuck in a million-dollar home with cut up women's clothes."

"At least she didn't leave you with a child who she decided wasn't good enough for her."

I look up at him. "Touché." I sit on the bench she has in the closet, leaning my hands on my knees. "What the fuck do I do?"

"First, we clean this mess and dump all the shit at her parents' house," he says. "Then we go into town and have a bite to eat. You know the rumor mill is already going into overdrive."

"So we go and pretend everything is okay?" I ask him as my chest gets tight.

"We pretend every single fucking day till one day it is okay, and no one will know but you." He looks at me. "I mean, you get drunk as fuck the whole weekend, but Monday morning, you get up and go to work, and it's business as usual."

I agree with him. "I'm going to fake the fuck out of this," I tell him as I get up. Unbuttoning my shirt, I peel it off my body, uncovering the ink on my arms. "She fucking hated my tats. Did I tell you that?"

He shakes his head while I continue undressing. "Oh, yeah, it's not professional, she said. She actually looked up laser removal. It should have been my first clue she was not the woman for me."

I scoff. "High and proper all the time. She didn't even like to hold my hand in public." I raise my hands while I rant. "And forget about kissing in public. Dude, she thought it was like we were shooting a porn."

"But you loved her."

"But I love her," I repeat, not saying it in the past tense because I love her. I fucking love her.

"People do crazy things for love," Walker points out as I nod my head, walking to my plain closet to pull out a pair of jeans and slide them on.

"Today, I love her, and tomorrow, I'll love her a little less," I tell myself. Walker nods and turns around. Walking out of the room, he leaves me looking around the bedroom at décor I didn't even choose. The custom canvas headboard, the mirrored side tables I wasn't even allowed to breathe on. I make a note to call the decorator tomorrow and have her change them. I thank fuck we never slept in the bed, or I would get rid of that, too. No way in fuck would I sleep in the bed after she fucked me over the way she did.

"Gabriel." I hear Walker yell from downstairs. I walk out of the bedroom and look over the railing. "We have incoming," he says right before the doorbell rings, and I hear voices coming into the house.

"Are we burning this shit down?" Brody asks. He's followed by Darla, who puts her hands on her hips.

"We are most certainly not burning anything." She looks up at me. "How are you doing, sweetie?"

"You will not fucking call him sweetie, Darla," Brody growls from beside her five-foot body. His six-foot-five frame making him even bigger. She walks over to him, reaching him mid-chest. "No," he says, putting his hands around her waist and bending down in half, "not a fucking chance. He has a name, so use it."

"I love only you." She laughs into his chest. "Gabe"—she looks up—"are you doing okay?"

I don't have a chance to answer her because more voices fill the room. This time, it's Grandma and my mother. "Okay." Grams puts her sunglasses on her head. "Let's get everything that isn't Gabriel's and pack that shit up."

I stand, looking down at my family, not saying a word. "We started in the bedroom," Walker says. "Well, he started in the bedroom." He points upstairs. "It's a massacre."

The women gasp and look up. "Did you touch the shoes?" Darla dares to ask, almost as if I told her I killed a puppy.

"All of them," Walker confirms, and Darla puts her hand over her mouth. "Every single one destroyed."

"You didn't," Darla asks in a whisper, and I think I see tears forming in her eyes. "Even the Manolo Mary Janes?"

"How the fuck am I even supposed to know what that is?" I ask, putting my hands on my hips.

"I would have bought those from you," she says, and

then Brody comes back with a roar.

"Over my dead body would you wear that woman's shoes."

"It's a shoe," Darla says.

"Then buy your own fucking shoes." He crosses his arms over his chest, and the fact his beard is long and so is his hair makes him look almost like a barbarian.

"Those shoes are nine hundred dollars!" She puts her hands on her hips, and then Brody's head whips up to look at me.

"You bought her nine-hundred-dollar shoes?"

"I was in love with her," I counter. "Can we focus on the fact that I was left at the fucking altar yesterday, and I'm hurt?" I try to pull the sympathy card, and it only works for the girls while Brody just glares at me. "What?"

He points at me and mouths, "That's fucked up." Even though I didn't think I would ever smile again, that makes me crack a smile. I didn't think I would ever have a reason to smile again. But now, looking down at my family who showed up to protect me from the storm, I have to have faith that tomorrow will be a better day. At least, I hope so!

Chapter Seven

Crystal

"You sure about this?" Blake asks from beside me when he finally turns off the truck. I look around at the houses that line the street, nodding.

It's been three weeks since Eric died; two weeks since his brothers came to the house and 'claimed' all his belongings. Two weeks since Hailey was served with papers demanding she cease and desist slandering Eric by insisting he married her.

As if she could forget she married him, that she loved him, that for that one minute, he wasn't really hers.

I get out of the truck, looking at the little gray house with flowers lining the walkway. The brown door with the hanging 'Welcome' sign. I look down at my feet, take a big deep breath, and then walk toward the house, Blake right behind me. I put one foot in front of the other until I get to the porch and reach out, ringing the doorbell. The sound can be heard from the open windows upstairs.

We hear footsteps coming toward the door. "Here we go." I open and close my hands, and my nerves start to get the best of me. My heart starts to beat even faster against my chest as the footsteps approach the door. I hear the lock turn and watch as the handle turns right.

The door swings open, and there standing in the middle of the doorway is the woman I came to meet. The woman with long, straight blond hair that lays over her thin shoulder. Her big brown eyes are too big for her face now, something that probably wasn't there before. Her clothes look five sizes too big for her. "Can I help you?" Her voice comes out soft.

"I'm Crystal," I say, my voice wavering a bit, but her eyes go big when she finally recognizes the name.

"We are sorry to just barge in on you," Blake starts saying when she looks at him. "We were wondering …"

Samantha moves out of the way. "Please, come in," she says as I walk in, followed by Blake. "Don't worry about taking off your shoes," she says to us as she turns and walks into her house. The entrance is closed in, and when we walk into the home, we both stop in our tracks. Pictures of Eric are everywhere; the pictures of his family cover the whole wall in the living room. Pictures of him and the girls scattered throughout the room.

Samantha turns around and watches us take in all her pictures. She points at the big portrait of the four of them. "That was taken the day we found out we were expecting our third child. Two weeks later, I miscarried." The picture hangs in the middle of the living room wall "Would you like to sit here or in the kitchen?"

"I can't sit in this room," I tell her. "It's just too much." She nods her head as if she understands.

I follow her into the dining room as she turns and goes into the kitchen. "Would you like something to drink?"

"Water," I say, my throat now dry. She goes to the fridge, opening the door, and we see the drawing on the fridge. "It can't fucking be," I mumble to myself.

She comes back, handing us each a bottle. "I don't know what the protocol is for any of this, so I don't want to be rude in any way." She crosses her arms over her chest.

"We just want to talk," Blake finally says, and she nods at him and walks to the table.

"I need to sit down." She almost collapses in the chair. I take a seat on the opposite side.

"Are you okay?" Blake asks her as her eyes fly to his while he takes a seat in the chair next to me.

"No, actually, I'm not okay. I'm the opposite of okay," she sighs. "I have to pick the girls up in an hour," she starts and places her hands on the table as she wrings her fingers.

"Did you know?" I come right out and ask the question, a question everyone must be thinking.

Her head shakes from right to left. "Not a fucking clue." She wipes a tear from her face. "How long were they together?" she asks, and I finally get it that she must have just as many questions for us as we have for her.

"They were married for the past six months but dating for about eighteen," I tell her the truth; it's not about lying, it's about fucking closure, for her and for us.

She nods her head. "I just thought we were going through a rough patch." She doesn't try to wipe away the tears this time. "I even felt him get distant, and we spoke about it." She sniffles as I listen to her. "He said it was all in my head."

"Do the kids know?" Blake asks, and she shakes her head.

"My in-laws will not permit me to tell them anything except that he died in a car crash."

"Your in-laws are not your boss." I sit straight up, my spine going rigid.

"I'm a foster child and grew up in the system. They are the only family I have, so they are not the boss of me, but they are my family." She sits up. "It is also none of your business how I handle *my* children."

I'm about to freak out, and Blake must feel it because he puts his hand on my arm. "You're right. They aren't my business, and you aren't my business, but my cousin, his other wife, is my business," I start, and I don't stop now, my voice getting higher and higher. "You had your fucking closure. You got to say goodbye to him, but she didn't." She glares at me, but I don't care. "She had to sit in the middle of her fucking living room, that they shared together, and read a fucking cease and desist letter, telling her that everything they had meant nothing. That is my fucking business."

"You done?" She has the nerve to ask, and I nod. "You think I had closure because I got to see him in a box? He was dead. You think just because I got his body that I got closure? You think it was easy for me to be the wife and mourn by his casket when all I wanted was to tell everyone what a fucking fake he was? If you think I got the better end of the deal, that is where you're wrong." She stands up now. "Your cousin gets to have the time to cry and ask questions, but I have to hide my pain and all my tears because I have two girls who I have to live for. I cry into my pillow at night quietly, so they don't get up and ask me, "Do you miss Daddy, Mommy?" when the whole time I don't fucking miss him. I fucking loathe him. He took our wedding vows and made a mockery out of them. He took me and made me look like a fuck-ing fool. Do I have his name, yeah, but I would give it back to him. The only thing I can't hate him for is giv-ing me my girls." She swallows. "When I look in their eyes, which are just like their father's, I can't hate him. So don't sit there thinking you know anything when you know nothing."

"We are very sorry," Blake starts, and she puts her hand up.

"Please, spare me the fake sorrow. I don't have the privilege to bash him and his ways because my in-laws hold him on a fucking shrine. I can't look at them and tell them what a piece of trash their son was because then I will be left by myself. I play the wife role; I take the well wishes of the people who come up to me, but at night, when all the lights are off, when the kids are tucked into their bed, I'm left picking apart every single memory I have." She raises her voice. "And it's a lot more than eighteen months."

"This was a mistake," I say softly, looking at Blake.

"You came here to see who I was, and I get it. I wanted to do the same. I wanted to meet the woman who he felt he loved so much he lied and married her. But I can't because, at the end of the day, those girls need me." Blake nods then stands, and I walk out of the house without another fucking word. I walk down the step, climb in the truck, buckle my seat belt, and look straight ahead.

"Well, that was a good idea," Blake finally says when we are far enough away. "Great fucking plan that was."

"She is more broken than Hailey is," I finally say out loud. "Hailey can forget about him, but she will never be able to move on."

"You going to tell her about this?" he asks me, and I nod. "When?" he asks the million-dollar question.

"When she can handle it. Right now, the only thing she can handle is her bottle of wine. It's got to fucking end."

He nods. "Give her another week." He stares ahead, not even bothering to look at me.

"Another week." I throw my hands up. "I don't give a shit what you say or that you're older than I am and wiser. Next week, tough fucking love starts."

"Deal." He looks over at me. "And I won't even give you a hard time about how you treated Samantha." I roll my eyes. "She isn't the enemy."

I don't bother to answer him. Instead, I close my eyes and devise a plan that I will put into place exactly one week from today.

Chapter Eight

Gabe

"Come in," I say when I hear the knock on my office door. I'm sitting at my desk going through resumes, looking for someone to replace Laura, my head nurse who took off with Bethany.

"Oh, son, I'm glad I caught you before you left," my father says, and I don't know if he's being sarcastic or not. I'm here at the practice every single night till at least nine o'clock. The house is just too much for me to take in right now. But it's getting easier. Once we got all of Bethany's shit out of the way, I called the decorator back to make a couple of changes. Luckily, she was able to exchange the things I didn't want, so now it's almost my style. Almost.

"I met with Alan this morning, and I think having him on as the pediatrician would be a great idea." I nod at him, thinking that adding on that part of the practice will be great.

"Walker's building a lot of new homes, meaning new families are moving to town. I think it's a smart idea." I agree with him. "But now you know that we are going to have to add a couple of nurses, right? I think I found someone to replace Laura, but she's from the city, so I don't know if it's a great idea. She will probably be bored out of her mind and then leave us high and dry."

He nods his head. "Yes, I was thinking of that." He puts his hands in the pockets of his white lab coat. "Son, you need to stop this."

I lean back in my chair. "What is that?"

"Staying here till it's dark, coming in on Sunday just so you aren't home. If you hate that house, sell it."

"I love that house," I tell him, and I really, really mean it. "It's my dream home."

"Then start living in it," he tells me. "Stop making it her house and make it your house."

"Dad, it's been two weeks," I tell him. "What would you do if it was Mom?"

"I'd chase her down and drag her ass back," he tells me. "Did you ever stop to wonder why you didn't chase after her?"

"Dad, she left me at the fucking altar. I'm pretty sure she was done with me."

He rolls his eyes at me, literally rolls his eyes at me. "But you never went after her. Doesn't that tell you something?"

"Yeah," I agree with him, "that I'm not a fucking doormat."

"Bullshit. If you loved her, like really loved her …

loved her so much your heart would stop beating if she was gone. Like you didn't think you could breathe without knowing you are going to wake up next to her every single morning. Loved her so much you would have followed her and fought her every step of the way, then we wouldn't be here." I don't say anything. "That is love, and if you felt that, you wouldn't just let her walk away." He nods at me. "Don't stay too late." He turns and walks out the door, leaving me with my thoughts.

"I love her," I tell the wall, but I think about what he just said, and then I think about the love he shares with my mother. There is no way he would have let her get far without putting up a fight. He would fight for her with his last dying breath. I think about Brody and Darla. If she left, he would basically go fucking caveman on her and literally build an island she wouldn't be able to escape from.

I stack the charts together, locking up and make my way outside to my truck. Not a car in sight in the deserted parking lot.

I look over at Walker Construction, which is just next door, and see the glow of the red sign. Not one car in their parking lot either. I make my way through the town where I grew up. I take in the shops and the hustle of town for almost seven p.m. on a Friday. I pick up my cell phone and call Walker.

"Have you eaten?" I ask him when he answers.

"It's seven o'clock, and I have a four-year-old. I ate at five like a senior citizen." He laughs at the last part.

"Okay. Mind if I swing by?" I ask him even though I

know I don't have to. I can just show up, and he wouldn't even care. It's always been like that.

"Like you have to ask." He chuckles. "I have to go. I just heard Mila ask why bubbles are coming over the bathtub."

He disconnects as I make my way over there. I open the door and head straight to the kitchen for a beer. I check out to see what leftovers he has and score big time when I find warm lasagna on the stove.

"Uncle Gabe!" Mila says, running out of the bath-room naked. "Daddy is lost in bubbles," she yells and then runs back in the bathroom. I follow her to see the bubbles everywhere.

"What?" I ask, seeing Walker try to swat the bubbles down. "I think you put too much."

"This is your fault," he huffs. "While I was talking to you, she emptied the whole jug of bubble bath into the bath." He looks at Mila, who shrugs and then bends to pick up the bubbles in her hands and blow them in the air. I watch him try to contain the bubbles for twenty minutes, and he finally plops Mila down inside the tub. I turn, going back to my lasagna while he bathes Mila.

Mila comes to kiss me goodnight while I flip through the channels on the television. Walker comes out ten minutes later and heads straight to the kitchen for a beer. He comes back to lie on the couch.

"You think if I really loved Bethany, I would have gone after her when she left me?" I ask him. He eyes me sideways, knowing I'm asking out of curiosity and not because I'm moping. "Dad said if I really truly loved her,

I would have chased her down."

"Well, I mean …" he says, taking a pull of his beer.

"So would that mean you didn't love Julia with everything that you have?"

"Bethany didn't have an affair with your best friend. She also didn't have a kid and not know who the father was. Julia didn't just leave me; she left her daughter. That is fucked up, and there is not enough love in the world to forgive that or to fight for it."

"Okay, fine, but do you agree with him?" I ask him, and he just shrugs his shoulders.

"I'm not saying I agree with him. I'm saying I think you would have fought harder."

I shake my head and turn back to look at the screen. I want to argue with him, but instead, I ponder the words in my mind.

I spend Saturday and Sunday working in my yard. My yard. Doing what I want to do. I call in the guys to add a pool. I walk through the rooms and make a checklist of what I want to change and what I'm going to keep.

When I finally pull into work on Monday, I feel refreshed. Debra, our receptionist, smiles at me when I walk in. "Good morning, Dr. Walker. How was your weekend?" Her smile bright on her face. She has been with my father almost since the beginning.

"It was great, Debra. What about yourself?" I ask as I walk past her.

"Great." She nods. "You have a full day ahead." I nod, walking back to my office. I open the door, dumping my bag. Slipping on my white lab coat, I grab my stethoscope and throw it around my neck. I walk out to the middle of the practice where the nurses' station is. It is almost like a hospital emergency room with the nurses' station in the middle and the examination rooms in a circle.

"Good morning," I tell the nurses who are all around sharing their stories of the weekend.

We have a total of five nurses with us. Emma usually works with my father. Olivia just started, and she usually handles the newer patients. Ava has been here for three years and is usually my go-to. If there is something I need right away, I give it to Ava.

Mia has been here the longest, and she works with all of them, making sure everyone is taken care of. Since she has the most experience, they usually bounce ideas off her.

Corrine works hard and plays harder. If I had to pick anyone who would try to hook up with me, it would be her. I, of course, would never put myself in that situation, especially after Bethany.

"Morning," they all say.

"I heard we have a big day ahead of us," I tell them, looking at the whiteboard with all the appointments listed. "Who is working with me today?" I look back at them.

"That would be me." Ava puts up her hands.

"Lost the bet, did you?" I smile at her, putting my hands in my pockets. I'm a hard person to put up with when I'm working. It's got to be go time every single time. The phone buzzes, telling us we just got an emergency walk in. "Let's go, people."

I clap my hands, getting ready for the start of the day.

The hours fly by today, so fast I don't think I even chewed my lunch. I finally pick up my phone to look at my messages, and I'm flipping through them when I see one from Theo, the medical equipment supplier.

Hey, we are having a medical convention in two weeks. It's from Monday to Wednesday, and your father already confirmed your attendance. See you then.

Great.

He knew I would have said no, so he went behind my back to my father. Asshole. I shrug off my lab coat and unbutton my cuffs, rolling up the sleeves. I sit down at the desk to begin finishing the paperwork from today, and it dawns on me that I didn't think of Bethany all day. Not once. I smile. It's going to be a great week.

Chapter Nine

Crystal

I buckle my seat belt and take off for Hailey's house. It's been one week since 'the outing,' and she hasn't collapsed in a heaping pile. All in all, I call it a success.

Walking into the house, I toss my purse on the couch and walk to the kitchen to find Blake, Hailey, her parents, and Nanny. "Hey, you guys." I make my way to the coffeemaker, pouring myself a nice hot cup. "Whatcha looking at?" I ask as I pick up a picture of a house. The house looks cute and quaint. I flip through the pictures, taking in the backyard, and see another swing, but then I see the ocean and the calmness of it.

"This is so pretty."

Blake fills me in on what was just discussed. "That is where Hailey is going to, as Nanny says, 'find herself.'" He uses his fingers to air quote. I nod my head, my eyes never leaving the paper as I take in the swing in the front. I sip my coffee while sitting at the table when Hailey mentions selling everything. I look up to find Nanny's eyes on me. We share a secret nod, and I know what I need to do. Nanny leaves when we sit down to eat.

I walk out of the house and make my way right to Nanny's house. It's no surprise she already has the coffee ready.

"Come in," Nanny yells when she hears me knock. I walk into the living room, ignoring all the pictures of the family, and find her in the kitchen. "Oh, you came?" She smirks at me.

"You think her leaving her family and her support system is a good idea?" I ask her, crossing my arms over my chest as I think about Hailey leaving here.

"She isn't leaving all her support system; she is still going to have you." She pours us coffee. "And the answer is yes, I think her leaving will help her because staying here sure isn't fucking doing anything." She hands me the cup of coffee.

"Who says I'm going with her?" I raise my eyebrows at her.

"You and her are glue … where one goes, the other goes. Even if Eric was alive and you left, she would follow you."

"I have a job here," I point out, and she just shoos me with her hand. "I'm not just going to sit by her side all day."

She gets up and walks to the counter, picking up a business card. "This is the number to Dr. George Walker, Delores's son. He runs a practice out there with his son." Nanny tells me about her friend Delores, who she has known since she was in her twenties. I flip the card in my hand as she finishes. "Give him a call."

I nod my head, thinking that if worse comes to worse, I can always see if anyone in the area is looking for an RN. When I leave Nanny's, I make my way home, but the decision is already made for me regardless of what happens when I call Dr. Walker.

The next morning, I walk into the emergency room with a letter in my hand. It comes as a surprise to everyone, but when they hear my reasons, they understand. When the chief of surgery found out, he offered me more pay to work with him. I smiled at him and turned him down, and then asked him for a reference letter.

So now here I am about to do my final interview with Dr. Walker.

My palms are wet as I press the Skype button.

The Skype rings, and two seconds later, the screen says it's connecting.

The man who comes on is an older gentleman. "Hello there." His smile lights up the screen.

"Hello, Dr. Walker." I smile and try not to stutter.

"I have about ten minutes until my next patient, but I don't think this is going to last long," he says, and my heart starts to beat uncontrollably. What does that mean? "I got your resume, but I have to say what impressed me most was the letters of recommendations."

I try not to smile too much, but I think I fail.

"I love what I do." I smile. "Not many people can say they wake up and smile when they go to work, but I'm one of those people."

"You got recommendations from every single specialist in your hospital. And they were all outstanding. Your chief of surgery, Dr. Mawlings, offered to buy me a very expensive bottle of scotch if I picked someone else."

I throw my head back and laugh. "Shepard has been trying to get me to join his team since I started there." I shrug my shoulders. "But I couldn't leave the emergency room."

"At this point, I think I should be the one trying to woo you." He laughs. "We would love to add you to the team. The job is yours if you want it."

I cheer on the inside. "I would love it."

"Perfect," he says. "Why don't we plan on you starting three weeks from now?"

"That is perfect. I already gave notice, so I could have even started in two weeks."

"There is no rush," he says as his phone buzzes. "I have to go, but I look forward to seeing you when you come to town."

"I can't wait to see what the Carolinas have in store for me."

"We look forward to showing you the beauty of it."

Once we say goodbye, I get up and head to my room to dress in my scrubs. When I walk into the emergency room, there is a spring in my step. "Seven days, peeps," I say. "Four more days and it's mic drop." I smile at Dawn, laughing when she flips me the bird.

"We are going to throw you a going away party." She leans back, yelling, "Don't make any plans on Tuesday." I nod as I head into the break room to put my lunch bag away. Dawn walks into the room. "What the hell are we going to do without you here?" she asks.

"Don't you fucking cry." I point at her, seeing the tears forming in her eyes. "I will cut you," I tell her. "And I'm a nurse, so I know exactly where to cut you so you bleed out and feel lots of pain." I blink away my own tears.

For the past year, it has been the two of us during every single shift. So many come and go, but Dawn, she was my go-to. Stuck, quiet, needed a break, or just wanted to step away for a second, she knew, and she gave me what I needed. I knew her also, her strengths, fear, quirks, and especially, what pissed her off, and I never, ever crossed her when she was pissed. The day flies by with a couple of gunshot victims and always that one drunk when we do rock, paper, scissors to decide who will take the case. She always does paper; I don't even know if she realizes she does.

When things finally settle down, I sit down at the nurses' station to finish all the files before shift change. "So you're really doing this?" Dawn asks from her side.

"Yup," I answer, not looking up. "I know she would do the same thing for me, no questions asked." Dawn doesn't say anything; she just hums her acquiescence.

The week flies by, and there is so much to do. I had to sublease my apartment, pack it all up, and help Hailey with her purge of Eric or, as she is calling it, 'shit for sale.' When Tuesday night rolls around, I'm more than ready to cut loose. I've already sent my stuff to the house, and I have one suitcase left. I had nothing to wear tonight, so I ran out at the last minute.

I shower, toweling down with a small tea towel. I pull up the light pink skirt, zipping the gold zipper in the back. I grab the strapless white top, which zips up the back also. The loose chiffon outer layer floats, leaving the white material underneath snug to my body. I pair the outfit with pink open-toe suede booties. My makeup is minimal; I plan to drink heavily tonight and having to deal with taking it off when I get home will be one less thing for me to do. I grab a shawl and make my way downstairs when I hear the honk of the Uber.

Walking out of the apartment building, I see Dawn waiting for me. "Holy shit, someone is getting lucky tonight." She snaps her fingers.

"One can hope." I wink at her, ducking to get into the car. We make it to the bar where we have spent many nights closing it down. It's where the hospital staff always goes. It's where every birthday, retirement, and going away party takes place. Pulling up, we see that the place is already busting at the seams. "Holy shit, are all these people for me?" I joke as I get out of the car and we make our way inside. If it looked packed outside, it's only a glimpse of what is inside. The four corners are almost all full.

"Crystal." I hear my name yelled from someone to the side and see half of the nursing staff of the emergency room all around a high-top round table. I grab Dawn's hand and lead us to the table. "Look at you," Harriet, the head nurse, says.

"Who ordered shots?" asks Patrick, the head of surgery, carrying a tray full of shots. "Look at you?" he says.

I roll my eyes. "Jesus, do I look that bad in scrubs?" I say. Picking up a shot of tequila, I down it, hissing at the burning down my throat. "Why is this place so packed?"

"Medical convention," Patrick tells me as soon as he swallows the shot.

Over the next hour, half the ER nurses and doctors show up, and we've taken over five more tables. After a couple of more shots, my smile is plastered on my face as people come over to me and tell me how much they are going to miss me. The people keep coming in and some leave, some linger. The music begins to play, so we throw our hands in the air and swing our hips.

"I'm going to the restroom." I giggle to Dawn, who nods her head at me. Making my way through the crowd of people around the bar, I bend my head to watch my feet. Walking into the dim hallway, I smash into a man who has just come out of the bathroom. His arm automatically flies to wrap around my waist and bring me against him. His smell intoxicates me further, and I giggle as I try not to fall. I put my head back, looking up at him, and my smile gets even bigger. "I'm sorry, I wasn't watching where I was going." I look up into his blue eyes, and he smiles down at me.

"It's my fault." His voice comes out deep. "I should have looked right and left when I walked out of the bathroom."

I throw my head back and laugh. "I get it. Like crossing the street."

He loosens his hold on me, and I step back, finally taking him in. His hair is cut short on the side, the top longer. His t-shirt looks like he is bulging out of it, especially his biceps. Ink decorates both arms to his wrists. His jaw looks chiseled, his nose perfect. I don't know if it's the booze talking or not, but this man is fucking perfect. "Are you here for the convention?" I ask him, and he nods.

"Are you?" He puts his hands in his back pockets.

"No, I'm a nurse over at the hospital," I tell him as someone walks by me and nudges me with their shoulder, sending me flying into him again. "Sorry."

"You've fallen into my lap twice now, and I still don't know your name." He smiles at me, holding my arms in his hands.

"I'm Jane," I tell him, hoping he gets the joke. "Jane Doe." This time, he is the one throwing his head back and laughing.

"Well, Jane Doe, I'm John." He holds out his hand, and I take it in my hand, shaking it. "John Doe."

"I think we're related somehow." I smile at him, and this time, his eyes go serious.

"I really fucking hope not." He takes a deep breath.

"I have to go to the bathroom," I say, dropping his hand. "Excuse me." I look down and then back over my shoulder once I walk away to see him staring at me. "Enjoying the view?"

"More than you fucking know." He smiles, and I push open the bathroom door, whispering, "Holy shit," the whole time.

Chapter Ten

Gabe

I watch Jane Doe walk into the bathroom, thinking this night just got a whole lot better.

When we first arrived an hour ago, even with a large crowd I spotted her. My gaze found her right away, and then she moved her hips, and I just couldn't look away. It was as if fate handed her to me when she smashed into me.

I look toward the bar and then back at the bathroom door as I list the pros and cons of staying and leaving in my head. Everything tells me this is a bad idea, but I go with my gut, which brings me back to the women's bathroom door. I lean against the wall, facing the door, one foot on the wall, and both hands in my pockets. I haven't done this in forever. I was never a one-night stand kind of guy, but something tells me not to walk away.

The door swings open, and there she stands. If I thought she was good looking through the crowds of people in the dim light, then nothing compares to her standing in the fully lit bathroom. Her blond hair falls down her back and her blue eyes shine with mischief. Her neck bare and white gives me the sudden urge to bite her. "You waiting for me?" she asks, walking to me.

"I wanted to know if maybe you wanted to grab a drink." Her citrus smell hits me in the stomach. Fresh and clean. "I was thinking," I say, tracing my finger down her cheek, "we could maybe go over our family tree."

Her hands go straight to my waist as she leans into me. "Let's go have that drink." She winks at me, walking away from me as I follow her to the bar. "What are you having?" She turns to ask me.

"Scotch on the rocks," I yell to the bartender, who then looks at her. "I'll have the same," she says.

"So." She leans in, the noise of the bar drowning out her voice. The bartender returns with the two scotches and places them in front of us.

"Put it on my tab," I tell him, and he nods his head. I pick up the glass, holding it in front of me. "To long-lost family."

She picks up her glass. "To living in the moment." I clink her glass in a toast, then she drinks a sip and looks at me. "Are you married?"

I shake my head. "Nope. Single. You?" I ask her. Even though I want to do this, I don't want to cross that line.

"Always single." She smiles, taking another sip, this time longer. "So, John"—she looks at me, stepping into my space—"there is just one more question that needs answering."

I down the scotch, not even hissing when it burns my throat to my chest and then straight down to my stomach. I place the glass on the bar. "Do you want to go some-place where it's quiet?" I ask her. She nods and smiles at me. It's a smile that I'm not sure I ever want to see go away. It's a smile that lights up her whole face. I don't know if it's the booze or not, but I'm not ready for it to be over just yet.

"I just have to tell my friends I'm leaving." She points behind her and goes to tell them something while I close up the tab. A couple of women look over her shoulder, waving their hands at me, and one high-fives her. She shakes her head, laughing, while she walks back to me. "So where to?" she asks me. I grab her hand and walk outside to the building next door. "Well, that wasn't too far."

I guide her to the elevator and press the button standing next to her. I'm nervous; I haven't had sex with someone new since Bethany and that feels like forever ago. I start thinking about different moves when the elevator dings, and the doors open. She steps in before me. "What floor?" she asks.

"Twenty-seven," I say, and she presses the button. She leans on the wall while I lean on the other across from her. "I don't usually do this."

The little minx smiles at me. "A one-night stand or sex?"

I smile at her. "Very funny. A one-night stand."

She stands straight and walks over to me. Her hands go straight to my chest, causing my heart to beat faster.

"Well, then"—she inches closer, her hands moving to my neck, and my hands going to her waist, pulling her close to me, "let me start then."

She goes on her tippy toes, and something in me takes over. I turn her so she is the one against the wall now. My hand runs over her bare neck, coming up to cup her chin. "I'm the one driving this car," I tell her right before I hear her breath hitch and my mouth crashes into hers. I taste the scotch on her when her hand touches my cheek, and I angle my head to get more of her. To get all of her. The elevator dings, letting us know we are on our floor. Our lips separate from each other as our chests rise and fall rapidly. I hold out my hand, and she places hers in mine. As soon as our fingers intertwine, I pull her out of the elevator before the doors shut us in. She laughs as she follows me, and I make the mistake of looking over at her, seeing her with her hair going everywhere, the smile on her face, and the twinkle in her eyes. I make sure to remember it all.

I scan my card, opening the door and pushing her against it when it closes. This time, she groans when I press her to the back of the door. My hands go down to grab her ass. "Fuck," I hiss when she arches her back and tries to push into me. My cock's harder than it's ever been; either that or the restriction of my jeans makes it seem that way. I lean my head down to suck her neck, her hands frantic on my shoulders, my back, and finally, my hair. She tries to spread her legs, but the tight skirt restricts them. So she pushes me from her neck, and when I swoop down to take her mouth again, she turns and her ass hits the desk. I frantically pull up her shirt, her hands diving under my shirt, the need to feel each other almost too much for words. Our mouths never leave each other, my hands going from the back of her thighs to her tits, then all the way to her neck. She rips the shirt off my body, our mouths leaving when she pulls it over my head. Tossing it over my shoulder, I reach for the zipper on the back of her top. A zipper that taunted me while she walked away from me. The sound of the zipper echoes through the whole room as she sits there on the desk with her legs spread open and me standing between them. My mouth wants to taste her more, so I lean down, taking her mouth again. The zipper slides down, her top falling on the desk when I get to the bottom, and I know I have to see her. My hands roam up her back, feeling her skin get goose bumps as she groans into my mouth and pushes her chest into mine. I leave her mouth, looking down at her perfect tits. Everything about this woman is perfect. I take a nipple into my mouth as my hand squeezes the other one; her nipple pebbles in my mouth as I bite down, and her head goes back. "I need."

Her hands reach for my waist, straight to the button on my pants. She unsnaps it while I switch breasts, the sound of the zipper drowned out by our moaning and panting. Going straight for my cock, she fists it in her hand, and this time I moan.

She pushes me off her. Getting on her knees, she drags my pants off my hips. Never missing a beat, she sucks my cock to the back of her throat. My hips move on their own, and my eyes close for a moment as I take in the heat and wetness of her mouth. Fuck, I love her mouth on me, and I love that she loves doing it more. She moans louder than I do when she takes me deeper and deeper.

She takes me the way she wants to, and all I do is let her. Once I feel my balls get tight, I pull back. I pull her up, turn her around, and unzip that fucking pink skirt to find there isn't anything under it. She looks over her shoulder at me, her hair ruffled and flipped to the side, her lips swollen from our kisses. I have tonight with her, and I'm going to fucking make sure she fucking remembers me for a long, long time.

Chapter Eleven

Crystal

The sunlight hits my face, waking me up when I turn my head, and I blink slowly. I'm lying face down, the sheets are white, and a soft snore comes from beside me. I turn my head to take in 'John.' He is on his back with one hand over his head, the other on his chest, and the white sheet covering the best part of his body. Don't get me wrong; his six-pack was a welcoming surprise, the ink on his arms and chest even more so, but his cock. I hit the motherload, and fuck, do I feel it today. I stretch out my body, tensing while I do it. I look over at the clock and see it's a little past seven. I sneak out of bed, trying not to make any sudden movements. When my feet touch the floor, I hear his moan beside me, so I stop, but he just moves his head to the other side. A soft little hickey has formed by his nipple, making me smile when I remember when it happened. I walk to the bathroom, bypassing the pile of discarded clothes. His jeans, my shirt, his shirt, my shirt, a wet towel, another towel, my shoe. I bend down, picking up the empty condom wrappers. We used a box of twelve, fucking twelve. I've never had sex like this. I've never *wanted* sex like this before. We did it fucking everywhere, giving in to every single one of our fantasies. I step into my skirt, zipping it up, then move to my shirt. My leg muscles scream at me; I guess squatting over his cock for ten minutes wasn't the best idea since I haven't worked out in forever, but I honestly felt like a porn star. That was right after the shower, or was it before he ate the whipped cream off me? I look in the living room area and see the uneaten strawberries, but the whipped cream is all gone, or better yet, it's smeared on the coffee table. I really hope they disinfect this whole room. I bend to pick up one of my shoes and tiptoe around the room to look for the other one. I look out the window overlooking the city … is that my ass print? I tilt my head—it must be—and right next to it are my handprints clear as day from when he took me from behind. I finally find my other shoe and bend to put it on.

I look back in the bedroom one last time, taking him all in. I will never ever see him again, and it kind of hurts that we don't even know each other's real names. But it was meant to be this way. I grab a pad on the desk that does, in fact, have more whipped cream on it. Grabbing the pen, I quickly write.

John,
You rocked my world, literally.
Jane Doe

I quietly open the door, holding it in my hand until I finally hear the click. I walk down the hallway with my head down as I pass the maids wheeling their carts for the start of their day. I smile at one of them. I'm not even sure I look halfway decent, but I don't really care because all I could do was play last night over and over in my head. It plays while I walk out of the hotel, while I flag down a cab, and especially when I climb into my bed. His smell still all over me, and he isn't the only one with wounds. I have his teeth marks right on my hips, where he bit me, and I smile at the memory. The guy was a beast in bed, and if we had more time, I would totally do it again. I fall asleep, only waking when my alarm rings at five p.m. I roll out of bed, and my vagina actually hurts. I haven't been that into sex in forever. Maybe the fact I knew I would never see him again added to the fact his penis was perfect and he knew how to use it like an expert. I just took advantage of it.

When I walk into Hailey's house an hour later, I smile at my family who have come together to say goodbye to her. She has no idea I'm leaving with her, so we say goodbye while she sheds tears, and I tell her I love her. I nod at Blake, right before I walk out to go back home for one last time.

The Uber picks me up right on time, helping me pack my two pieces of luggage. I text Blake I'm on my way.

We pull up right when Hailey pulls away from hugging Blake. "You came back to say goodbye," she says, wiping the tears from her eyes.

"Pfft," I blow out, smiling. "As if I would let you

leave without me," I say, going to the trunk to help the Uber driver.

"What is this?" she asks me as Blake grabs my luggage and puts it in the backseat.

"This is me and you taking on the world," I tell her, smiling as I wipe tears from my own eyes.

"You can't come with me; you have a job here," she tells me as Blake laughs, and she turns to glare at him.

"No, I had a job here. Now, I have a job there." She just blinks at me. "I left my job, but good news, I got one in town. It's a family practice. No gunshot victims and no stabbings, so it will be a walk in the park."

"You're coming with me?" she asks me, shocked.

"Of course, I'm coming with you." I roll my eyes at her.

"B-but," she stutters, "but we had a goodbye dinner last night."

"Well, it was a free meal. How would we not?" I tell her as I grab my last bag from the Uber. "So what do you say, should we start our new adventure?"

She smiles at us then looks down at her feet nervously. "I have to lock up the house. Um, if it's okay, I'd like to do this on my own." We don't move from the street as we watch her walk inside the house and say goodbye to her memories. Blake leans against the back of the car.

"You guys going to be okay?" he asks, and I lean next to him.

"I think so, but it all depends on her." I shrug my shoulders. "She decides she wants to come back, we come back."

"What about your job?" He looks over. I shrug my shoulders again. "Will you tell her about Samantha?"

"Yes." I rest my head back. "When she's ready." We look up when she comes out of the house with tears streaking her face. I rub her arms while she gives Blake the keys to her house. "Good thing I'm coming. Who else would drive?" I tell her and walk to the car to give them the chance to say goodbye.

She climbs into the car, buckling up, and leans her head on the window looking outside. "Isn't this just like Thelma and Louise?" I ask, and she laughs.

"Can we do it without the whole driving off the cliff or shooting Brad Pitt?" she asks me as I pull up the Waze traffic app and follow the directions.

"I say we still shoot Brad Pitt but don't die either. I mean, imagine if one of us survived without the other." I shake my head as she leans her head on the cold window. "I'd come back and haunt you. Just saying." She laughs and closes her eyes as I proceed to the directions. We don't talk much. Both of us finding out we start back at work in four days. Hailey is a web designer, so she will be working from home.

After four hours of driving, we stop to get gas and use the bathroom. Hailey grabs some food for us, and we get back on the road for the rest of the journey. Having both windows down allows the country air to settle in with us as the mountains in the distance get closer. We turn off the interstate at our exit, the full trees lining the street on both sides, and we follow the directions, turning once to go down Main Street.

Passing over a little bridge, we watch the creek on both sides, the water flowing down. Once we get off the bridge, I see every single shop has the American flag hanging outside. As we slowly roll down the street, I look at all the shops. The sidewalk consists of tiny red blocks. The bank sits right next to the post office. I see two cop cars parked right in front of the police station.

A guitar hanging outside the fourth building makes me know it's a bar.

"I think everyone knows everyone," Hailey comments as she looks at her side of the street. "We should take a walk tomorrow night," she says as I turn left in the front of the pharmacy, which just has the mortar and pestle on it. We pass the courthouse, or at least it's what I think it is because it has courthouse written in the middle of it.

We continue down and pass what looks like a cul-de-sac with two houses on the street. We turn down a gravel road, and I take in the lush trees on both sides as we get to the house. The white house looks deserted and nothing like the pictures.

"What the fuck?" Hailey says what I'm thinking. I put the car in park in front of the house. I open my door, going around to the front of the car, and I see a shutter that looks like it's falling down. *Motherfucking*, I think to myself.

"That picture lied." I grab my phone to call Nanny right away, and not surprising, it goes to voicemail. "I know you're not answering because you know why I'm calling." I don't even say goodbye. "Maybe it's just the outside." I dig in my purse for the key Nanny gave me last night. "Let's go and see how bad it is." We walk up the front steps and find one whole step missing. Missing a fucking step. I look up at the sky, praying for fucking patience. I'm cranky, I'm tired, and while my body still aches from my sex marathon, it's asking me to go back for more.

I shake my head as we make it to the door, turning and seeing that swing that stood out in the picture. The chains that hold the swing are rusted and covered in spider webs. The wicker seat is so dirty, and the pink rug that was under it is blown half over. "Okay, so we need to do a couple of projects," she says as she puts the key in the door and turns the lock. "Well, at least we aren't locked out." She opens the door and takes a step in.

The huge living room is empty. Just a single white chair in the middle of the room faces the fireplace that has a board nailed in front of it. The gray floor has seen better days. I turn the lights on, but they just flicker. We walk in to see the kitchen to our left with a wooden island in the middle and all the cabinets white and sterile. The only thing with color is the brown wooden butcher block counters. The deep white porcelain sink faces the window looking out to the front. The windows have no shades. The white gas stove with black burners has seen better days as has the fridge. Making my way to open it, I'm accosted with the smell of rotten cheese mixed with some eggs and god knows what the fuck else. It smells worse than the fucking morgue. "We need to buy a new fridge and stove," I tell her. I hate to be the one always thinking negatively, but this is the worst shit ever. When

I get my hands on my grandmother, I'm going to throttle her.

I follow Hailey down a hallway, rolling my eyes at the bathroom, and then see the bedroom with access to a closed-in back porch. It almost gives me the creeps, so I don't fight with her when she calls dibs. Besides, I need to be away from noise when I sleep.

I head to the living room and walk up the stairs, where we find two more bedrooms with a huge bathroom with a sunken tube. After we walk to the back of the house, I pick my room, and Hailey decides to make the third bedroom her office. "Fuck. Where the hell are we going to sleep tonight?" I ask as we walk back downstairs.

"We are going to sleep here," Hailey says as my phone rings.

"Nan, you have so much explaining to do," I start off and then walk around the empty room.

"I just got your message. Is the house not to your liking?" she says.

"It's empty," I tell her. "Like so empty I don't even think racoons would live here," I continue as I walk to the back of the house.

"You were always so dramatic. I'm sure it's not that bad."

I roll my eyes. "Yeah, yeah. Well, you'd better call your friend and tell her that we need the super or someone to come and clean this shit up."

"Okay, fine, I'll call Delores and have her come see you. Now make the best of it."

I press the end button. "I don't think there is a super."

I look at Hailey, who stands there smiling. "We need to hit up a Walmart or a Target." I open my maps and google the closest Walmart. There must be a mistake, so I refresh again. "What the fuck? The closest Walmart is an hour and four minutes away."

Hailey nods her head and smiles, then heads outside to grab our bags and bring them inside. "An adventure," she tells me, and I glare at her. If I could, I would growl at her. Not only am I sleeping on an air mattress, but I also have to hit up a Walmart. Someone kill me now; I pray this is the only hiccup I have while I'm here.

Chapter Twelve

Gabe

I pull up to the clinic and slam my car door. I walk in without a word to anyone. I just nod, walking back to my office. I've just gotten back into town from the conference.

The conference where I met the hottest chick of my life and had the best sex of my life. Multiple times, so many times I thought my dick would chafe. Only to wake up to an empty bed, warm strawberries, and a goodbye note. I don't even fucking have her name. Jane fucking Doe. I grab my white lab coat, and I'm putting it on when my father comes in smiling, and it irritates me. "Hey, son."

"Yeah," I grumble.

"The new nurse starts on Monday; just giving you a heads-up."

"Did you hire that one from the city?" I ask, grabbing my stethoscope to put around my neck.

He nods his head while I shake my head in disbelief.

"I think it's a big, big mistake."

"Is everything okay?" He puts his hands in his pockets. "You look angry."

"No, it's fine. I'm just tired. I got in late last night. I'll be fine." I smile at him and then walk out to the nurses' station. "Okay, what do we have?" I ask them, and they tell me where to go. The day drags by or maybe it doesn't. I don't know; the only thing I think about is Jane, or whatever her name is. I am about to kick myself in the ass when I walk out of examine room three, heading to the nurses' station, and I hear that laugh. My whole body goes on alert; my feet stop moving, but my cock springs into action as if he knows. Turning the corner, I see the back of her, and I know it's fucking her. The question is, what the fuck is she doing here? My father looks over the woman's shoulder. "Oh, great, Gabriel, come and meet Crystal. She was next door and decided to pop in and introduce herself before she starts on Monday" It happens in slow motion, just like in the movies. She turns her head, her hair flying with her, and then I see her face. The face that has haunted my dreams for the past two nights.

Her eyes widen when she finally sees me, and I see she is just as affected as I am. I make my way to her, holding out my hand. "Pleasure to meet you." I smile at her the whole time I'm fighting with my body; my brain says one thing, but my cock says 'it's go time.'

She puts her hand in mine as I shake it harder than I want to. "Nice to meet you, Dr. Walker. I'm Crystal." Everyone is looking at us now as we smile at each other and our hands go up and down.

She finally pulls her hand from mine. "I'm excited to get started," she finally says, looking around.

"I'm sorry." I tilt my head at her. "You look like someone." I watch her throat move up and down as she swallows.

"I don't think we've ever met." She smiles and then looks at my father.

I tap my lip with my forefinger. "Nope, wasn't you. The girl was Jane," I say as she smiles while her eyes glare at me.

"Well, I'm glad we got that out of the way." She turns to my father. "It was lovely to meet you, and I look forward to working with you on Monday." I don't say anything, nor do I reach out and drag her back to my office to talk, or taste, or fuck against the door.

She waves goodbye to everyone and stops to talk to all the nurses on her way out.

"Where did she come from?" I turn to my father, who is watching me.

"Your grandmother's friend Sheila, the one she met at one of those senior getaways." he says as I nod. "That's her granddaughter."

"Oh," I say softly.

"They are renting Walker's house."

My eyebrows pinch together. "What do you mean, Walker's house?"

"Well, the white house," he says, looking down and then up. "I have to go. Your mother is waiting for me."

"Holy shit," I say under my breath; she is living in the

white house. I pull out my phone to call Walker.

His answer is gruff. "So how is your day going?" I ask, knowing it's probably shot to shit.

"I just left *your* grandmother's house, who, by the way, thought it was a good idea to rent out my house to two fucking chicks from the city." He always calls her mine when she does something wrong, which knowing our grandmother is something huge.

"Really?" I say, turning and going into my office. "Which girls?"

"How the fuck should I know? I just want them out, but one of them came down here and threatened to sue me when I laughed and told her to fuck off. Gram also thought it was a good idea to invite them to live with her till I fix the house."

"Wait a second." I try not to laugh at him. "Gram rented away the house of torture?" My laughter finally escapes me.

"Fuck you," he says right before he hangs up, and I laugh louder. Shaking my head, I take off my lab coat and go to the computer, opening it up to the employee records. I type in Crystal's name, but nothing comes up. They probably haven't entered the info yet. I get up, going to the front desk. "Hey, Debra, by any chance do you have the file for Crystal, the new nurse starting Monday?"

She picks up some files and then finds the one she is looking for. "Here it is, but there isn't anything in it yet."

I nod. "No worries," I say, going back to my office. I try going by the rental house and see no one there. The next day, I drive to my grandmother's and find the house empty. I try later that night, and they are still out. What the fuck?

I'm on my way home when the phone rings, and I see it's Brody. "What's up?"

"I need your help tomorrow, please," he says. "We just finished the remodel at Walkers, and well ..."

"Nope, not happening." I don't even listen to what he has to say.

"Gram said if you said no, she is going to get you here one way or another, so I'm not sure how you feel about that."

"Fuck you. I don't have a choice now, and you know that."

"See you tomorrow. I'll pick you up at eight. Besides, you get to meet your new nurse. I haven't met her, but Doug said she's hot as fuck."

"You need to tell Doug to go fly a kite and not fucking touch my staff members." He doesn't even answer; instead, he just laughs out loud, and I disconnect him. The next day, Doug arrives right on time. I throw on my oldest jeans, t-shirt, and baseball cap.

"Good morning, sunshine," Brody says when I climb into the truck. I just grunt at him while he drives us to the house. We arrive, and I hear Brody yell.

"Ladies." All the women there turn around—my grandmother; Walker's mother; Darla, Brody's wife; Crystal; and who must be her cousin. "This is my best friend, Doug." Doug just nods at us as Brody continues the introductions. "This is Kingston," he says of the middle one. "Now, this one is Gabe." He looks at Crystal. "And her boss." He points at me, and my hands go to my hips. "Can we finish this today, please? I have a shit load of stuff to do this afternoon." My voice comes out harsher than I wanted it to as I jump into the back of the truck and begin unloading the boxes. It takes us three hours to unload most of it, and the last pieces are the second bedroom set. "That one is for the upstairs bedroom." Doug smiles, grabbing one side of the headboard while I grab the other side. I walk up the steps to her bedroom and find her standing in the middle of the room looking out the window.

"Where do you want us to put it?" Doug asks.

"Right in the corner diagonally," she says, gesturing in the direction with her hands.

"You can't have it that way. You are going to lose all kinds of space," I tell her as I place it down against the wall. Doug walks out of the room to head back downstairs.

"You can't tell me where to put *my* bed in *my* own room." She puts her hands on her hips, hips that I grabbed when I pounded into her. I shake my head to clear the memory.

"I can't tell you anything apparently." I slap my hands together. "Don't leave the bed like this; you will get more use out of the space."

"Last I checked, this was my bedroom. Therefore, I can put my bed where I want."

"You know what? This isn't going to work." I put my hands on my hips. If she is this hardheaded about a bed,

I can't imagine how we would work together. "You're fired." As soon as I say the words, I know I've made a mistake.

"I'm what?" She glares at me. "Oh, fuck no. I'm not fired because guess what?" Pulling out her phone, she dials someone on speakerphone as I look at her and she glares at me. My father answers right away.

"Hello?" he says, and Crystal starts.

"Dr. Walker, I'm sorry to do this to you, and it may be unprofessional of me, but I can't work with your son."

He laughs and then asks, "What did he do this time?"

"Well, he came into my home and demanded that I follow his rules. I simply can't work in that type of environment."

I open my mouth in shock that she just blatantly lied. "LIAR," I mouth.

"I'll take care of it," he says as he hangs up. My phone suddenly rings, and it's my father.

"Hello?" I say, glaring at her while she turns her hand and looks at her nails.

"I don't know what you did, but you'd better undo it," he hisses.

"Dad," I try, but he ignores my pleas and continues.

"She is going to be the best thing to happen to that nursing staff in forever, and I will not let you and your craziness turn her away." I look back at Crystal who is almost tapping her foot. "Be nice," he says then he disconnects.

"Are you okay?" she asks me. "The vein in your forehead looks like it's going to explode. Do you need medical attention?"

I swear I'm going to throttle her. Right after I kiss the shit out of her.

I turn and storm down the stairs, out the door, and straight to Darla's car. I'm really fucking glad the keys are in the ignition, so I start it up and get the fuck out of here. What the fuck was I thinking? From now on, no more thinking of that fucking night. She works for me and nothing else. Easy, I can do this. I head to Walker's house because he'll know what to do. When I pull up and go inside, I find Mila on the couch watching *The Boss Baby.*

"Uncle Gabe!"

"Hi." I smile at her, going to kiss her head.

I walk to the kitchen, open the liquor cabinet, take out a glass, and down a shot. "What's gotten into you?" I pour myself another two fingers. Once the burning fades away, I hang my head. "So are we discussing this, or are you just going to sulk in the corner?" he asks, and I glare at him.

"I just met the woman replacing Laura," I tell him as he whispers, "Oh."

"Yeah, that," I say, going to sit on one of the stools. "Plus, she lives in your old fucking house."

"Don't even fucking think about it." He points at me. "She doesn't need you sniffing around her just to add another name to that list of yours."

I look at him with a confused look on my face. "What the fuck are you talking about? What fucking list? You know Crystal?"

"Oh, her." He crosses his arms over his chest. "I thought you were talking about Hailey."

"And if I was?" I ask him now, my eyebrow shooting up.

"Why are you so pissed about it?"

"She wants to put her bed in the middle of the room. Diagonally," I tell him, gesturing it with my hands. "Who does that? We would never be able to work together so I fired her."

"So you fired her?" he asks me, folding his lips and trying not to laugh.

"Yes, but then the little … the little," I try to come up with a name, "the woman called my father and quit."

He doesn't even try to hide his laughter as he belly laughs out loud. "It's not fucking funny. He took her side."

He puts his hand in front of his mouth and gasps. "Shocking?"

"Fuck you, Walker," I say. "I knew she was fucking trouble from the moment I got her application. She comes from one of the top hospitals in the US. She was even given a reference from the head of surgery, who called and begged me to turn her down." I get up, getting more scotch. "I told my father to turn her down, that it wasn't a good idea, but then Gram came in, and it was a done deed."

"Why would she want to leave a big hospital for a small medical clinic?" he asks, but then the oven beeps and he goes on dad duty. I sit at the counter with Mila eating fish sticks with her. When Walker goes to give her a bath, I sit on the couch and watch *SportsCenter*. And as I fall asleep on his couch, I hear her moans in my dreams.

Chapter Thirteen

Crystal

The alarm goes off at six a.m., and I groan. I was so nervous about starting my new job today that I didn't get to bed until way after two a.m. Rolling out of bed, I step in the shower, finally waking up when the cold air hits my ass. I grab my blue scrubs and slip them on, feeling like going home. I grab my white Nikes and slip them on, too. I put on a coat of mascara and pin my hair on top of my head.

I try not to make noise when I make my coffee and toast and grab things to make lunch. The hot coffee hits my tongue first. "I would give up sex I think for coffee," I tell myself. "Okay, not sex. Maybe after-sex conversation."

The toast pops up just as Hailey storms into the kitchen ranting and raving about a dog who bit her. I roll my lips together when she mentions the asshole neighbor.

"Okay, I have to go." I pick up my bag, looking at her.

"You have bail money saved up in case, right?" Grabbing the keys to the car, I walk out and make my way over to the practice.

I get there, and the parking lot looks almost full. I grab my stuff, take a deep breath, and pull open the door. The lady greets me with a huge smile. "Good morning," she gets up, coming to me. "You must be Crystal." She holds out her hand. "I'm Debra."

I shake her hand. "I'm excited to be here." I smile at her as she opens the door to the back.

"You can go on into the back, someone will show you around."

"Thank you," I tell her, smiling at her. I turn and walk back to the center of the nurses' station where I find four nurses standing around talking about their weekend. The blonde one looks over at me. "Hey."

"Hi there, I thought I would be the only early one." I smile at them.

"Are you kidding?" the blonde answers. "Mia is here a good hour before we start. She makes us look like we are always late. I'm Ava."

I nod. "I'm Crystal. Is there a staff room or employee fridge or anything?" I ask them, and the one who I think is Mia comes forward.

"I will take you." She turns, and one of the other nurses follows us. "Emma," she asks the nurse who followed us, "is the locker near you taken, or is it still free?"

"It's free," she says. "Come on, I'll show you." I follow her into a small room filled with light brown lockers against the wall. "This is the changing room; showers and the bathroom are through that door." She points at the side door on my right. "That door"—she points to my left—"leads to the kitchen."

"That's easy enough," I tell her. "Which one should I put my things in?" I ask her, looking at the lockers.

"The one at the end isn't taken; it was Laura's." She raises her eyebrows, and I know there is more to the story. But I don't ask her. I place my bag in the locker, then take out my stethoscope, and put it around my neck.

Turning with my lunch in my hand, I walk to the kitchen. I'm surprised by its brightness; back at the hospital, we had a corner, and you were lucky if you found your lunch when it was your turn to eat.

Windows line one wall, causing the green tiles to pop from the natural light. A table sits in the middle of the room with a huge bowl of fruit on it. "Dr. Margaret Walker, the Mrs., brings in fresh fruit every Sunday. She usually only comes in on Fridays to take care of some of the older patients," she informs me as I look around.

There is a Keurig on the counter and a huge stainless steel fridge. I open the fridge and find it almost empty. "The fridge is cleaned out every Saturday, so if you leave something in it, too bad. It's tossed out." I nod, taking in all the rules. "The coffee pods are all stored in that cabinet, help yourself whenever you like." I smile at her.

"Thank you so much, Emma, for taking the time to show me around."

"I'm going to go use the bathroom before the shift starts," she says, going into the room. I turn to grab a water bottle out of my lunch when I hear voices coming into the room.

"If he would give me the time of day, I would make sure he forgot all about being left at the altar," Ava says, pushing open the door. "Sorry, I didn't know anyone was in here." She smiles, and there is something about her that I just don't like. You know what they say ... smile and wave. I also see that I have landed in grand central gossip. As a former nurse in an ER, there was only one thing we loved more than doughnuts, and that was knowing the latest gossip, and oh was there ever gossip.

"I was just getting my water bottle," I tell them with a smile. "So have you guys worked here long?" I try to be friendly.

"I've worked here three years, and Corrine just started six months ago." She points at the other brunette.

"I'm excited," I tell them.

"You should be. You get first dibs with Gabe today," Ava says, and my eyebrows pinch together. "He always works with the new nurse for about a month before we go into rotation again. He needs to get a feel for how you work."

"Really?" I say, taking a sip of water. She is about to say something else when we hear a beep on the intercom. "Let's rock and roll, girls." I follow them out to the nurses' station. The six of us stand around while Mia talks.

"This is the patient roster for the day," she says, pointing at the whiteboard. There are three columns: Dr. Walker, Sr., Dr. Gabe, and Emergency. The whole day is filled up, so at least it won't be boring. "Since it's Crystal's first day, Mrs. Walker is stopping by to bring lunch."

"High five," Emma says to herself.

Mia begins discussing the day when I see Gabe walking out of his office. The lab coat fits snug around his biceps. Watching him from my peripheral vision, I notice his eyes find me, then look away.

"Good morning, everyone," he says, looking at the whiteboard. "Going to be a smooth day, right?" He smiles at us, and I want to do two things. One—roll my eyes, and two—I want to feel his lips again. I shake my head. *Bad idea, Crys, bad fucking idea.*

The intercom beeps again. "Go time, people. Crystal, you're with me," he says, walking to a room. I follow him and see that he is going to his office. "Since we didn't have a chance to talk about your experience and stuff, I think it's good if we discuss how we work."

I cross my arms over my chest. "Are you the type of doctor who is going to be leaning over my shoulder?"

He leans against his desk, crossing his legs, and I swear his package looks like it's bulging. "I'm the type who is going to be watching to see if we are a good fit. I need to have confidence in my nurses."

"I have no problem with that. I feel the same way," I tell him. "Do you want me to get to the patients before you come in, or do you want to be there when I get their information and their vitals?"

"To begin with, I'll be in there with you, and then we will see how it goes."

"Perfect," I tell him, nodding while his phone buzzes and we hear Debra's voice.

"Um, Dr. Walker, Bethany is on line one." If I thought

the vein in his head was throbbing yesterday when we fought, it's nothing like now.

"You can go ahead and get started. I'll be right there," he tells me, not moving from the front of his desk. I nod and walk out of the room.

I look at the whiteboard when I walk back out and see that I have a patient in room two. Grabbing the chart, I walk into the room to a middle-aged woman who is texting away on her phone. "Good morning," I greet her as she looks up. "My name is Crystal."

"You're the new one?" she asks, and I just nod.

"That I am." I place her file down. "Are you here for any particular reason?"

She looks down and then looks up again. "Nope, just a follow-up. I had my physical last week, and the results came in."

"Perfect." I smile at her. "I'll just take your blood pressure while we wait for Dr. Walker." I wrap her arm with the inflatable cuff. "It's one ten over seventy," I tell her, documenting the measurement in her chart. The door opens, and Gabe comes in.

"Hello, Mrs. Brewster, how are things?" Gabe starts as I hand him the chart. He takes it, nods, and opens it up. "All your results came back normal, so unless things change, you can come back in six months."

"Well, there is something I think we should discuss. Ever since menopause started, I'm not really in the mood." She looks at her hands and then up. "And before, I was, well …" She tries to search for the right word.

"Active?" I help her try to find the word, and she

smiles.

"Yes, I was active, very active. But now it's …"

"I see," Gabe says. "I can prescribe you Addyi. It's the female version of Viagra."

"Yes," Mrs. Brewster says as Gabe writes her a script. He hands her the paper as she thanks him and walks out.

"Go start in room four." His voice is soft, but he doesn't look up while he writes his notes. I walk out, and for the rest of the morning, it's almost as if we work in sync.

Until we get an emergency call and I rush out to see that Hailey is carrying Mila in her arms, her feet bare and bleeding. "She got hurt," Hailey says, trying not to move Mila, who whimpers.

I open the door for her. "Someone get Gabe." I look over as Hailey follows me. "What happened?"

"I was sitting outside eating an apple because my eyes were hurting from the computer, and I saw her and that fucking dog playing." The tears pool in her eyes. "She got hurt, but she was so brave." I move around her, taking in the weird angle of her arm. "I think it's her shoulder or her wrist." It's definitely broken, and the way her shoulder just lays there, I would say it's dislocated also.

"Hey, Princess Mila, you think I could see what is wrong with you?" I try to not give away anything while Hailey talks to Mila, and I take in what I thought all along. I take her wrist in my hand lightly as she cries out.

"Look at me, Princess. Just … I know it hurts, but I promise you she will make it all okay." Hailey tries to calm her down, but now the tears are falling down her face.

"Don't cry, Hailey," Mila says. "I won't cry if you don't cry." I nod just as Gabe walks into the room.

"What is going on?" he says as he takes in Mila on the table. "Where did all this blood come from?" he asks, and Hailey looks at him confused, and then looks at the floor and sees that the blood is from her feet.

I've worked alongside some of the top doctors in the states, but working along Gabe is even better. He swings into motion. "We are going to have to pop the shoulder back into place." He looks at me as I nod.

"I think her wrist is broken." He nods at me.

"Your cousin is going to need stitches on her feet." We work around it until Mila's father comes in and treats Hailey like a second-class citizen.

"Okay, folks, I have to put her shoulder back in place." Gabe looks over at the man who I found out is called Walker, when he showed up at Norma's spewing shit, "It's going to hurt, and she will cry, but there is nothing we can do about it." I stand on the right of Gabe when Hailey starts asking Mila questions, so she doesn't look at what he is doing. With one snap, it's back into place.

"You can go now. She just needs her family, not a stranger." Walker says to Hailey, who doesn't look at him.

Gabe orders an X-ray, and I'm listening to him when Walker dismisses Hailey without a second thought. I walk Hailey out with her feet bleeding all over the floor, and her shoulders slumped.

"I guess your daughter gets all her manners from her

mother," I hiss right before she walks out of the room to the sound of Gabe whistling.

"What the fuck were you thinking?" I ask her as I pull gloves on and walk over to her, picking up her foot. "I need to clean this up, and then see if there is any more glass in there. I'm guessing not, but you can never be too sure. You will definitely need stitches."

I clean up her feet when Ava walks in. "Gabe was calling for you; I'll finish here," she tells me as I take off my gloves and toss them in the trash.

Finding Gabe in the hallway, he looks at me. "You ever do X-rays before?" I almost roll my eyes at him.

"Yes, Dr. Walker." I nod. Going into the examine room, I tell Mila we will be doing X-rays and lead her out to another room. The whole time I remain professional and don't tell her father that he's a fucking douchebag.

"You are a champ, Mila." I smile at her as she nods and asks me about Hailey. "She needs stitches, but she is going to be just fine. How about we get you all better?" Finishing up with Mila, I walk back out to see Gabe talking to a woman and smiling. "X-rays should be done, Dr. Walker," I tell him as the woman approaches me.

"You must be Crystal. I'm the third Dr. Walker." She holds out her hand, and I now see the resemblance. This is Gabe's mother.

"So nice to finally meet you." I smile at her, holding out my hand.

"Word on the street is that you've hit the ground running." She puts her hands in her pockets and smiles. "I hope we get to work together soon."

"I do as well," I tell her and then excuse myself to take a breather. Walking to the nurses' desk, I pick up my water bottle, draining it.

"Crystal." I hear my name being called. "Room four," Gabe says, and I walk in with him. He looks at the X-rays and tells us what we already know. I help him cast Mila's arm. By the time they leave, it's almost four o'clock.

Mia and Emma have already punched out, and Olivia's coming out with her lunch bag. "There's the city girl." She smiles at me. "I hope to see you in action more often. It was great seeing you just fly around and handle the trauma without a second thought."

"Thanks," I tell her as I walk to the nurses' station. "Now the best part of the day. Chart follow-ups."

Ava and Corrine are the next ones to leave. "Want to come have drinks with us?" Ava asks.

"Thanks for the invite, but I have about an hour of charts left, then I should go home and check on my cousin." We say goodbye, and I return my attention to filling out the charts. What was supposed to take an hour takes much longer, and when I look up, I see it's almost fucking six.

"Fuck," I say when I see Gabe walking in, surprised to see me.

"What are you doing here?" he asks.

"Charts," I tell him, looking down at the last chart. "I should be done in about five. Do you want me to leave these charts in your office for you to look over?" I don't look up at him, and he tells me yes.

Walking into his office five minutes later, I see he has

taken off his white lab coat and sits behind his desk looking through charts. "Here you go." I hand him the pile. "If that's it, I'm gone."

"I get it," he finally says right before I'm about to walk out the door. "Why Dr. Mawlings didn't want to let you go."

I cross my arms over my chest. "Are you giving me a compliment?" I ask, my eyebrow shooting up.

"Take it as you want to." He looks down. "See you tomorrow." I turn to walk out the door, something lingering, but I chalk it up to being tired.

Chapter Fourteen

Gabe

It served me right for waking up in the middle of the night on Walker's couch after storming out of the house because of how Crystal wanted to put the bed. I walked out and was surprised to see that Darla had come to get her car and dropped off mine. I tossed and turned the rest of the night and knew I would end up with a throbbing headache as soon as I started my day, and boy, I wasn't wrong.

"Good morning, Debra," I tell her, walking back to my office. I noticed that Crystal was already there, stepping into the nurses' station, and calling her back to my office, I didn't know what the fuck would happen. The last time I saw this woman I wanted to throttle her. But seeing her in her blue scrubs and black Crocs with her hair piled on her head, the last thing I wanted to do was throttle her. Then my day got a shit load worse. "Um, Dr. Walker, Bethany is on the phone." My stomach sinks, and I nod at Crystal to leave.

Picking up the phone, I grip it like my life depends on it. "Hello," I say gruffly.

"Gabe," she whispers, "um, I didn't think you would take my call."

"Well, I guess we are all surprised. What do you want, Bethany?"

"Well." She clears her throat, and her voice returns to normal. "First, I was wondering how you were doing?"

I laugh out bitterly. "You mean from when you left me at the altar with five hundred of our closest friends and family? I'm doing fucking fantastic."

"Gabe," she says, "I'm sorry."

"What do you want, Bethany?" I'm tired of the bull-shit right about now.

"Well, they gave me your account, so I just wanted to let you know that I'll be your representative from now on." We learned the day after she left that Bethany took a job from one of the pharmaceutical companies as their representative.

"Great, fantastic, I'll spread the word. Oh, and you'll deal with my father from now on."

"Gabe, we can still work together," she says softly.

"Oh, we can, I just can't stomach looking at you or hearing your voice for that matter. I'll let my father know. Take care." I hang up the phone without even giving her a chance to answer. I don't want her answers; I want nothing from her. I get up and walk out, looking at Ava. "Where is Crystal?"

"She is already in with Mrs. Brewster." She smiles at

me as I turn to walk in the exam room. I look at her notes in the chart, perfect and precise. We work side by side perfectly for the rest of the morning, and I know now why she was so highly regarded. She is the best you can get. And when Mila comes in with an emergency, I get to see her spring into action. I don't know if the other nurses would have cut it. She was two steps ahead of me by the time I finally walked in to see Hailey.

"There she is, wonder woman." I smile as Crystal glares at me. "Hey"—I raise my arms in surrender—"I'm not the bad guy."

"Whatever," she says as she gathers the supplies to start the stitches.

"How is Mila?" Hailey asks me as Crystal prepares to give her a shot to numb it. "Motherfucker, that hurts."

I watch her with perfect hands. "She's fine. Listen, about my cousin," I start to say, but Hailey raises her hand to stop me.

"Don't even bother." That's all she says because then she starts to hiss under her breath while Crystal works on her foot. I walk out of the room and see Ava.

"Can you finish the stitches on Hailey? I need Crystal to do Mila's X-rays." Nodding her head, she walks into the room, and I see Crystal walk in the exam room and lead Mila down the hall to perform the X-rays.

By the time the afternoon finishes, the headache I had at the beginning of the day is still lingering, so I sit down to check my emails and find an email from Bethany. I just forward it to my father, explaining what happened this morning. I also CC Debra on it so she knows not to transfer her to me. I get up to get some coffee, and I see that Crystal is still here, soft music coming from her phone. She remained professional all day, calling me Dr. Walker and never once slipping. Now I watch her as she turns, walking out and leaving me with the charts she just handed me. I check her notes, and I'm not surprised to find I don't have to add anything in. Everything is point form and perfect.

"Fuck," I say to myself, leaving right after her to go home.

Getting to the clinic the next day, I see Crystal sitting behind the desk with Ava, Olivia, Emma, Mia, and Corrine. "I can't believe you guys never did team building." She looks around.

"What are we discussing?" I ask them.

"Crystal's emergency team used to do team building exercises," Olivia fills me in.

"It just helps the team to work together," Crystal points out. "Know your weaknesses and your strengths and it helps your co-workers to jump in to make it better."

"That sounds like so much fun," Emma says. "I would totally do it."

"What about this weekend?" I suggest, not expecting them to accept. "We could go camping. In the wild."

Corrine looks at Ava. "Tent or cabin?" they ask at the same time.

"Cabin," I say, definitely cabin.

"Are we really going to do this?" Corrine asks.

"I mean, I'm game if you guys are." Crystal looks at

me. "I mean, Dr. Walker doesn't look that much like a camping kind of guy." She smiles big as the other nurses look at me, almost like she's baiting me.

"I camp." I throw down and hope to fuck my father doesn't come in right now and tell them that they had to pick me up when they sent me away to sleep-away camp. I was fucking nine, and it had rained nonstop.

"Do you?" Crystal says, getting up from the chair. "I'd like to see that," she murmurs under her breath, and I don't have time to counter because an emergency comes in. Mrs. Peterson fell in the shower and is now being transported to the hospital with a fractured hip. Once she came in, Crystal was there front and center, putting on gloves, and was one step in front. But when Mr. Murphy came in, that is when it started.

"What seems to be the problem?" I ask him.

He looks down at his lap and then up again as Crystal finishes taking his blood pressure. "All good," she says.

"Well, you see," he starts saying, "it burns when I ..." He lowers his eyes and then back up again, and I sit on the stool in front of him, waiting. "When I pee, it burns."

I grab his chart and see he's just turned thirty. "UTIs are very uncommon in young men," I tell him while he looks down at his hands.

"Well."

"Have you had anal sex lately?" Crystal asks as my eyes pop almost out of my head.

"Um," I try to say.

"It's not uncommon to get a UTI when you have anal sex and the cavity isn't clean." Crystal looks at Mr. Murphy.

"We tried it last week," he whispers. I sit here shocked while Crystal hands him a cup for a urine sample.

"Totally normal," she says, and he looks up with a sigh of relief. "All we need is a little sample and you can be on your way."

She smiles at him when he gets up and goes to the bathroom.

I wait for the door to close. "How in the fuck did you know that?"

She shrugs her shoulders. "It was common in the city." She leans over. "If you ever try it," she whispers, "use a condom."

Her hair falls a little on the side, her face free of makeup, her scrubs molding her … who the fuck knew that scrubs could be so sexy?

Mr. Murphy comes in carrying his sample, and Crystal puts on gloves when she takes the sample from him. "I'll be right back," she says, walking out.

"Besides the burning, is there anything that seems to be bothering you?"

"That was it," he says when the door opens.

"So it's positive," Crystal says, coming in, smiling.

"I'll prescribe you something." I nod at him, take out my pad, and write the prescription. "There you go. It's an antibiotic for ten days."

"Thank you so much." He smiles, grabbing it. "And for not making it awkward." He looks over at Crystal.

"Anytime." Crystal smiles, watching him walk out. "That was fun."

"You like this, don't you?" I cross my arms over my chest. "One-upping me?" I walk closer to her, and her smile turns into a smirk.

"It's not my fault you don't know the signs of men and UTI or"—she leans into me—"that you don't know about anal sex."

I push into her. "Make no mistake, I'm fully aware of the ass." Her breath hitches. "In fact"—I twirl her hair around my finger—"I seem to remember turning a certain ass so red, I'm surprised she was able to sit the next day." I press her into the wall. I don't know what the fuck I'm doing because I never even kissed Bethany in the office. But something bigger is pulling me. With her looking in my eyes, her chest rising and falling, I frame her head with my hands. My head just has to dip to taste her lips—they're right there. I can feel her breath on my lips, and I'm that much closer to having her lips on mine. Her breath hitches, and then my phone rings. We both snap back, the spell broken.

"I have to …" she says softly, walking out of the room. Looking down at the phone in my hand, I see it's Bethany, so I send it straight to voicemail and then block her number.

"Fuck," I say, rubbing my hands into my hair. "That can't happen again," I vow to myself.

Chapter Fifteen

Crystal

I walk out of the room and head straight to the bathroom with my head down. Closing the door behind me, I fall back on it, letting out the breath I'd been holding since he pushed me against the wall. Since he came so close to me I could smell his aftershave, so close I could almost taste him. One move, it would have taken one inch for my lips to touch his.

Walking to the sink, I turn on the cold water, never looking up. If I look up, I'll probably see my cheeks pink from the heat that spread through me the minute he mentioned smacking my ass. I shake my head, trying to push the memories of that night away. Except I can't. It lingers there, replaying every single time he moves next to me. Every time I see his hands, I remember the fingerprint marks he left on my thigh. I cup my hands to fill it with water and splash it on my face—one, two, three times.

This time, I look at myself in the mirror, and the pink

hasn't gone away. Turning back, I grab a brown paper towel to wipe my face. "Get it together," I whisper to myself, tossing the paper into the trash can.

Opening the door, I come face to face with Emma. "Are you okay?" she asks, and I nod. "Good. Dr. Gabe. is looking for you."

"Thanks," I say, going to the board to see what room he's in. My hand wraps around the door handle, and I take a huge breath. Opening the door, I see him on the stool with a little girl on the table, sitting on her mother's lap.

"This is my nurse, Crystal," he tells them while he looks in the little girl's ears. Her pigtails, perfect ringlets, her blue eyes crystal blue. She gives me a gummy smile.

"Hello." I smile at the baby and then at the mother who looks like she hasn't slept in three nights. "Aren't you the cutest?"

"Oh, she is, except when she decides she is going to sleep most of the day and party at night." She leans down to kiss her head.

"One ear looks a little red," Gabe says right when the little girl pulls at her ear. "Has she run a fever of any kind?"

The mother shakes her head. "Nothing. She is perfect except for the not sleeping through the night."

I grab the file and open it to see that she is about seven months old.

"She could also be teething." I look down. "Sometimes when these little angels start teething, they like to pull on their ears."

"Really?" the mother asks, and Gabe looks over with a raised eyebrow.

"Yes, it's pretty common with teething. Besides, she must have drooled right through that bib around her neck."

The little girl claps her hands, saying, "Dada, dada, dada."

"I'm going to hold off giving her anything for the next couple of days, but I want to see you in two days to make sure the ear isn't pinker." He smiles at the little girl, and my heart drops and sinks. I picture him with babies of his own, and it's too much.

So I do what I do best; I disconnect myself. I watch from afar as he says goodbye to the mother, and when he rubs the little girl's cheek, I turn away. I smile and wave at them when they walk out, and once they are gone, I open the door faster than my heart is beating.

"You okay?" he asks with his hand on my lower back.

"Yeah." I walk forward so I don't feel his touch. "It's just warm in here today," I tell him, walking to the desk to grab my water bottle.

"Can someone check the thermostat please?" Gabe yells from his spot, looking over at me. My eyes go to the desk, and I avoid his stare.

For the rest of the day, I never make eye contact with him again. We make our way from patient to patient, and I'm one of the first ones to leave. Getting home, I turn the car off, leaning my head against the headrest and closing my eyes. When my heart finally slows down and my breathing returns to normal, I get out of the car. Walking into the house, I yell, "Lucy, I'm home!" and put my bags on the table. No one answers me, so I walk to the back bedroom and don't find her there either. I walk to her back porch, and there she is, sitting in the swing with her legs stretched out as she watches the waves crash into the shore.

"A penny for your thoughts," I say, and she turns around. "You look a million miles away."

She shakes her head as she rubs a tear away. "Just thinking," she says. I walk over to her, picking up her feet and placing them on my lap as I sit down. We don't say anything as we both watch the waves. "You know, if you think about it," she starts, her eyes never leaving the water, "the signs were all there that something was going on." She laughs a hurt laugh. "All there … I was just too blind to see."

"If you were blind, then I guess we all were. None of us suspected anything." I squeeze her leg.

"But you guys didn't live with him." She inhales. "I was such a fool."

"No, you weren't." I try to get her to see, but she shakes her head.

"I hate him, like with my whole heart. For as much love as I had for him, I have just as much hatred." A tear slides down her face. I always wondered when I would be able to tell her about Samantha, and at that moment, with her doubting her whole life, I know this is the time.

"Hailey, you trusted him. You did what anyone else would have done." I rub her leg as she stretches her arm out and lays her head on it. "I went to see her," I whisper.

She finally looks at me, but this time, I look back at the water. "I didn't want to tell you … I just." I take a deep breath, and then look back at Hailey. "We went down and saw her."

"We?" she asks, confused.

"Well, Blake wasn't going to let me go by myself, just in case I did something harsh." I shrug my shoulders. "I just wanted to know, in case you had questions later. She …" She looks at me, and I let go of the tears I was holding all day, the tears that I'm shedding for my cousin, for her pain, and for my empty future. "She is so different from you. She isn't strong like you are. He's all she has ever known. She had no idea. She didn't suspect for one minute that he would do that to her, that he would do that to his family. He always traveled for work, so it wasn't like a red flag or anything. The only thing that changed is that the FaceTimes got less and less at the end."

"They have kids." I don't know if it's a question or not.

"Yes, and every single day, she has to look into the eyes of her children and see the good in them, or else she is going to go insane." I wipe the tears away. "That is what she has to live with. I wanted to hate her, to blame her for what he did to you, to us, but she had fewer answers than you did."

"I can't even imagine. I hated her," she starts to say. "I hated that she had that with him. That she had him forever. That their love would go on forever in their children."

I laugh sarcastically. "It was a lie. As much as you think your life was a lie, so was hers." She nods, and neither of us says anything as we watch the water go from dark blue to black as the sun sets and nighttime blankets the sky.

My dreams that night are nightmares. Even with the sun shining in them, I see a little girl running on the beach, her feet being swallowed by the waves crashing onto the shore. Gabe runs behind her, pretending to chase her, then picks her up, and flips her upside down. While her laughing and squealing bounces off the crashing waves, he looks back at me, his eyes pure happiness as he tells her something, and she waves at me. I sit there and watch him walk away from me, holding his little girl's hand. Getting farther and farther away from me.

My eyes fly open in a panic, and I lie here in the bed, blinking to take in the darkness of the room. I look over and see it's almost time for me to get up anyway. So I lie here, thinking about nothing.

Entering work the next day, I'm carrying a box of doughnuts. "Hey, guys, I was up super early and picked up doughnuts," I tell everyone. Walking past them to the staff room, I find Gabe making coffee while he checks something on his phone. "Morning," I say more chipper than I planned to. "I bought doughnuts."

He turns his head to look at me, his eyes roaming my body. "Thanks," he says, picking up his coffee and heading out of the room.

I grab my stuff and walk back to the nurses' station, seeing a picture of a huge log cabin. "What is this?" I look up to see Ava and Corrine smiling big.

"It's our cabin for the weekend," they tell me. "Dr. Walker cleared the schedule for Friday, so we drive up

Saturday and then come back Sunday."

I look down at the picture. It looks huge. "How many bedrooms?" I ask.

"Five," they both say together.

"Someone is going to have to share," Ava says. She looks around, and seeing it's only us, she says, "I say we pick straws to see who gets to share with Dr. Walker?"

I look up at them as Ava and Corrine nod, giving each other high-fives. "I'm out," I tell them. "I'll gladly forfeit that one."

"Are you crazy?" Ava says. "Not only is he so hot, he bought her the best shoes of life. I don't know how his fiancée left him at the altar."

My head whips around. "What?" I ask, trying not to be too eager, my heart pounding against my chest. "I …"

"Oh, yeah," Corrine says, looking around again. "He was up at the altar, and everyone walked down but her. Word is that she got some cushy job up in Chicago."

"I would not let him out of my sight if he was mine," Ava says. Corrine clears her throat quickly, so she stops talking.

"Where is everyone?" Gabe stops by my side, looking at his watch.

"They went to get a doughnut," I tell him. "So we really doing this whole camping thing?"

"We are," he says, watching Ava and Corrine get up and walk away. I turn to look at him.

"This should be a barrel of laughs." I wink at him and turn on my heels, ready to greet my first patient of the day.

Chapter Sixteen

Gabe

The knock on the door makes me raise my head from the charts in front of me. "Come in," I say. The door opens, and my father enters.

"Hey there." He comes in, going to the chair right in front of my desk. "So what is this whole camping retreat?" He folds his hands together, smiling at me. "You hate camping."

I lean back in my chair. "I don't hate camping," I tell him, and he raises an eyebrow at me. "What?"

"I just think it's funny that you're planning to take six women with you camping when you don't even know how to fish."

I roll my eyes. "I know how to fish. I just choose not to."

"Well, this should be interesting. How is Crystal?" He looks at me, and I know that his question is innocent.

"She's great."

"She already has all the other nurses on their toes." He laughs. "Emma said that Ava is not happy she isn't your go-to anymore."

"What is she talking about?" My eyebrows squeeze together. "I haven't treated her any differently."

"Not what she said," my father starts. "Just that Crystal is always the one you turn to now."

"I'm training her," I counter, "and she knows her shit, sometimes better than I do. She diagnosed a UTI because he had anal sex." My father throws his head back and laughs. "I wish I was kidding."

"I can't wait to work with her," he says, and something in my chest tightens. It's only normal he would work with her; she is a nurse. "So when do you guys leave?" he asks.

"Friday at six a.m.," I tell him, making a note to call the guys and see if I can borrow some camping clothes.

"Bethany called me today," he says, and I start rocking in my chair.

"Did she?"

"Yup, wants to come in and show us the latest things they are working on."

"When is she coming?" I ask him.

"Friday afternoon." He smiles. "That should be a good time. Your mother is going to sit in the meeting with me also."

"You think that's a good idea?" I ask. My mother is as prim and proper as they come, but Bethany fucked with her boy.

"I think that it's exactly what she needs to do. That

or"—he pauses—"she told me I would sleep on the couch for a week if I didn't tell her. Gotta say, not too fond of that fucking couch."

I laugh at him. "I don't feel you there." He gets up, knocking his fist twice on my desk.

"Now, go home," he tells me, and I nod at him, picking up the last chart to find I have nothing to add to it. Crystal is fucking efficient; I will give her that. I pull out my phone when I walk out of the office and call Brody, who answers on one ring.

"Do you have any camping clothes you can lend me?"

"Sorry, you lost me at you and camping." He laughs.

"Fuck off. I'm doing this team building bullshit, and we are going camping."

"Are you bringing tents?" he asks.

"Are you insane? I rented a log house. That house is a palace."

I laugh, getting into my car. "Can you help or not?"

"Sorry, buddy, you're on your own," he says, hanging up, and I make my way to the mall an hour away. I'm walking into the sporting goods store when I see someone to my right. Looking up, I watch as Crystal walks in. I've mostly seen her in scrubs with her hair tied up on top of her head, but now her hair is loose and wild. I speed up to her, scaring the shit out of her when I tap her on the shoulder.

"You almost gave me a fucking heart attack," she hisses. "What the hell, Gabe?"

"Sorry, I didn't mean to." I hold up my hands. "I didn't mean to. What are you doing here?"

"I'm picking up clothes for our camping trip," she tells me. "What about you?"

I look down and then up again. "Same."

She throws her head back and belly laughs. "I knew you didn't fucking camp. Liar." Shaking her head, she turns around and grabs a cart.

"Oh, shut up," I tell her, walking next to her. "This is all your fault."

"My fault?" She points at her chest. "Why would this be my fault?"

"You came in with your team building bullshit, and if I didn't jump on it, I'd be a pussy." I put my hands in my pockets as we walk slowly down the aisles.

She stops when she gets to the plaid shirts, looks for her size, and tosses two in the cart. "You didn't try them on," I tell her, and she shrugs.

"I don't need to. They're my size." She stops when she sees a vest jacket. "Should I get a jacket, or will the vest be good enough? I think I need some thermal underwear."

My hands fist in my pockets, thinking of her in any type of underwear. Fuck, if thermal underwear isn't turning me off her, then I have no idea what will. She fills her cart with clothes, and then we stop by the men's section. I grab a couple of flannel shirts, a jacket, a vest, and some long johns. "I think I need boots," she says.

"Yes, me, too," I tell her as we walk to the shoe department. She tries on a pair, and fuck, she can work anything. I choose mine, and we make our way to the cashier with her stopping and picking up a beige men's sweater with black symbols on it and a collar that folds down.

"What size are you?" she asks as she goes through the rack.

"A large," I tell her, and she tosses it in the cart. I look at her, trying to hide my smile "You buying me a gift?" I ask her, smiling.

"Not a chance in hell. You're paying for it; I just chose it." She walks toward the cashier and puts her things on the belt. She pulls out her card to pay for her things, then waits for me. I grab my bags and follow her out. "See you tomorrow," she says, walking to her car.

I'm about to call her back and stop her from leaving, but I don't. I watch her get in the car and drive off. I get into mine and follow her all the way home. She turns off before my exit, so I know she will get home safely. The next couple of days fly by, and then the big day is here. I get out of bed, groaning as I get dressed. I pick up a pair of jeans, a white t-shirt, and the sweater that Crystal chose. I put my blue boots on, picking up my bag. We are all meeting at the log house at six. I pull up with fifteen minutes to spare and see that I'm not the first one here. Crystal beat me here. She sits on the front step, and her pure beauty stops me in my tracks. She is wearing sunglasses, so I can't see her eyes, but I see what she's wearing when she stands. She is wearing the boots that we bought together paired with black leggings that mold to her long legs. Her shirt is a white plaid shirt, and she has the blue vest over it. The shirt stays unbuttoned, revealing a tight gray shirt underneath. Her hair is loose and the front tied back. "Hey," she says, coming to me.

Her citrus smell stops me in my tracks. "I got here ahead of schedule," she says, and I pick up my own Ray-Ban glasses. "Nice shirt." She smiles at me and crosses her arms over her chest. I don't answer her because another car pulls in, and I see that the other four carpooled.

"We made it," Emma says, getting out of the car. "Mia had to bail; her son got sick." Olivia, Ava, and Corrine get out of the car, stretching their legs.

"Shall we go inside?" I ask them, pointing at the house. I made sure to have the food stocked before we got here. We all walk up the six stairs to the front door. When I open it, I'm stopped in my tracks. This place is fucking huge and definitely does not fit in the camping category.

The whole house is wood, and in the two-story entryway, a staircase on the left side leads upstairs. The huge living room has a U-shaped couch facing a fireplace with a huge flat-screen television above it. The girls walk around me. "This kitchen is bigger than my whole apartment," Olivia says as I take in the stainless steel appliances and big wooden table to the side of it. A hallway to the left of the kitchen leads to the two downstairs bedrooms and a bathroom.

"We have two rooms downstairs and three upstairs," I say as Olivia, Corrine, and Ava all run up the stairs.

"There is a hot tub outside on the porch upstairs," one of them yells. Emma turns to go upstairs to look.

"Which room are you taking?" I ask her as she goes to the fridge. Opening it, she grabs a water bottle. "You want one?" she asks me.

"Yeah," I say to her. She hands me one as the four women come from upstairs.

"Now that Mia isn't here Ava and I won't have to share a room," Corrine says. "Emma is in love with one of the beds up there, and Olivia chose the one with all the windows."

"Guess that leaves us downstairs," Crystal says, looking at the girls and then me. "I'll take the one closest to the bathroom."

I nod and then a knock on the door makes us turn around. Emma walks to it and opens it, seeing a man there. "Hi, folks, are we ready to build us a team?" he asks, all gung ho.

"I have to change my shoes. I'll meet you guys out front," I tell them, grabbing my boots. I change out of my sweater, putting on a plaid shirt and a vest. When I get outside to the group, I see that the guy brought two other men, two good-looking men. One of them is talking to Crystal and standing way too close to her for my liking. She, on the other hand, is laughing away. "Are we starting?"

"My name is Paul, and this is my son, Luke." He points at the blond, who salutes us. "That is my other son, Holden." He points at the one standing next to Crystal. "First activity we are going to work on is communication. You will be paired up, tied at the wrist, and you have to find clues in order to solve your puzzle."

Emma snatches Olivia while Ava snatches Corrine, who looks like she would have bolted for me, leaving me with Crystal. "We left five clues around. The first clue leads to the next and so forth. The first team to win gets ten points, second five, and then the third team gets no points."

Luke ties our hands together with a blue rope, leaving just enough room between us. "You guys ready?" I look over at Crystal and then off we go. I have to say it is a fucking disaster. We can't agree on which side to take; I say right, and she says left. I pull on her, and she tries to kick my shins when I am walking. It is safe to say we come in last place.

"I want to change my partner," Crystal says as soon as we get back to base, leaving me all alone. Corrine jumps at the chance, and this time, I don't have to be tied to anyone. It is a scavenger hunt to find things. We all set off, but my eyes never leave Crystal as Holden follows her around everywhere. He smiles at her and the whole while I glare and don't even pay attention. No surprise we lost.

Corrine looks over at me, after we lost. "You suck, Dr. Walker." She walks back to Ava and tells Crystal that she wants to switch back. This time, it is a group challenge. There is this huge ball tied into knots. We have to stand around in a circle, and each person has a minute with it, and so on until it is all undone. This, I can do. We form a circle and start picking it apart, slowly at first. I can't get a knot undone, and I fucking hate it. The girls roll their eyes at me with frustration, and at one point, I want to take the fucking thing and set it on fucking fire.

"Not too bad," Peter says when he gets all the ropes back. "Just under ten minutes. We are going to break for lunch and get ready for the afternoon hiking session."

I turn and walk back into the house, the lunch spread I ordered all ready. We sit down to eat. "How is this fun?" I finally look at Crystal. "This whole team bonding is going to kill us. I thought Emma was going to stab me when I couldn't get that last knot."

"I wasn't going to stab you, Dr. Walker. Rip it from your hands, yes, but not stab." She smiles at me, and I just shake my head.

"Maybe it won't work here, but back when we did it, we found out what our weaknesses were and when to ask for help."

I shake my head. Not even bothering with this conversation, I'm praying I somehow break my foot or something just to get out of here.

Chapter Seventeen

Crystal

"It's beautiful, isn't it?" Holden says from beside me, and I swear if I could push him off a cliff, I would. He has been following me around the whole day, and I honestly can't stand him. At first, I thought it was cute, but bottom line, if you're a fucking idiot, I can't stand you. I look over my shoulder, watching Gabe talk with Ava and Corrine, who are just yapping away. They sometimes giggle and even feel the need to touch him. Dude, he's your boss. "So you think you can sneak away tonight?" he whispers, leaning in.

I tilt my head to the side. "Nope, sorry." I turn back around to see Gabe staring at me. "Are we almost done?" I ask, huffing and puffing.

"Just about. We have about another mile to go." He turns around, shouting to everyone. "About a mile to go, folks. Then you are on your own for the night." When we make it back to the house, all of us head to our respective rooms, and I grab my shower stuff. Making my way out to the bathroom, I run right into Gabe, who is carrying his own shower things.

Everything falls to the floor in one big pile. "Shit," I say, bending down with Gabe following me. I pick up my pants, top, and shampoo, and Gabe somehow picks up my panties. My very lacy panties. "Those are mine," I tell him. He holds them in his hand, and his head snaps to the hall entrance.

"So you *do* wear panties?" he asks with a twinkle in his eye. I try to snatch them from him, but he holds them from me. "I was dying to know."

"Well, now you do, so give them back to me." I open my hand so he can place them in my palm. He reaches over, and his fingers grace mine as he places them in my hand. "Thank you," I whisper, looking down at the floor. "Were you going to shower?" I ask him. "I can wait."

"No, it's fine. Go ahead," he tells me. When I look up, his eyes have the same look he gave me when he had me pinned to the wall in the office. It was the same look he gave me when he slid into me while he pressed me to the shower. I walk away from taking a shower, my body on high alert. I go to my room and remain in there until it's almost dinnertime. I put on another pair of black leggings with a big black sweater that falls off one shoulder and pin my hair on top of my head.

"What are we having for dinner?" I ask Emma, who is sitting at the island sipping water.

"Actually, Luke and Holden are going to take us out. Did you want to join us?" she asks me.

"I'm actually beat," I tell her, looking in the fridge. "Worst case, I can make myself a grilled cheese." The doorbell rings, and I hear the three other women come down the stairs in full makeup and all dressed up. "You guys packed heels?" I smile at them as they all say yes.

Luke and Holden walk in both dressed almost like they were this morning; their eyes pop out of their heads when they see the girls all dressed up. "I think this is going to be a short night," Emma says from beside me. "At least for me." I cross my arms over my chest. "You sure you don't want to come?"

I shake my head. "I'll be fine. You go ahead. Have fun, girls." They wave goodbye to me while I go to the fridge and hear Gabe coming from the back room forty minutes later.

"Where is everyone?" I turn to look at him. He's wearing track pants and a t-shirt that leaves his arms on full display.

"They went out on the town with Luke and Holden," I say from inside the fridge.

"And you didn't join them?" he says, sitting down at the island while I'm still poking around the fridge.

"Nope, a night in a dust barn doing line dancing isn't my cup of tea," I finally say. "What are we going to eat for dinner?" I ask him, closing the fridge.

"It's fully stocked." He looks at me, getting up and opening the fridge. "What do you feel like eating?"

"Grilled cheese and tomato soup," I tell him as he shuts the fridge.

He opens a couple of cabinets, taking out cans of

soup. "Your wish is my command." He smiles at me. "I'll make the soup; you make the grilled cheese. See? Team building." I roll my eyes at him.

"Fine," I say, getting the bread and the cheese out. "Did you want American cheese or another type of cheese?" I ask him while he looks for a pot.

"Anything," he says. He leans down, taking a pot out, and puts it on the stove. "So why didn't you go with the girls?"

I shrug my shoulders. "I just wasn't feeling it." I take some butter out of the fridge. "Um …" I say, stuttering.

"What's the matter?" He turns, looking at me.

"Nothing." I shake my head. "It's nothing."

"I don't believe you," he says, opening the can and pouring it into the pot. "What were you going to say?"

"Okay, fine," I say, buttering the bread. "You were engaged."

He nods. "I was, not too long ago."

"I heard she left you at the altar." I'm not sure if I'm asking him or telling him.

"I see the gossip mill is spinning," he says, stirring the soup, adjusting the temperature.

"So when we met in the bar," I look down, buttering the bread, "it was a rebound."

He stands with his back to the counter, his hip cocked out, folding his arms over his chest. "I mean, I get it."

"What do you get?" he asks. "I wasn't looking for sex that night. I wasn't looking for anything. But," he shrugs, "it worked out better than I thought it would." He smiles at me and my heart starts to beat up.

"How long were you two together?" I ask him and swallow. My stomach is starting to fall.

"Four years," he says. "We met in college right when I got accepted into medical school."

"That's a long time." I look at him.

"It was and I thought I knew her," he stirs the soup again, "I guess I was wrong." He looks up again. "I knew that she didn't like country life, but I thought she would somehow get used to it."

"But if she didn't like it here, why didn't you move?" I ask him.

"Because this is where I've always wanted to be. I graduated Harvard at the top of my class. I could have gone anywhere, but this is where I always wanted to practice. This is where I want to raise my family. This is where I'm meant to be."

"Are you okay?" I put the knife down to look at him.

He puts the temperature a bit higher as he stirs it, then turns to look at me. "The truth?"

"Of course," I tell him.

"I am," he says, crossing his legs at the ankle. "I wasn't." He crosses his arms over his chest, his biceps bulging. "I thought it was me."

I shake my head. "It's not you," I tell him, and a smile comes over his mouth.

"You'd better stop there, or I might think you like me." He pushes off from the counter as I roll my eyes.

"Like you? I tolerate you," I tell him.

"Really?" he says, coming to stand next to me. "When I stand next to you, I see your heart speed up." He uses his finger to rub down my neck exactly where my pulse is. "Right here."

I move my neck sideways to get him away from me. "I just …"

He moves closer to me. "You just what?" His palm is now cupping my neck.

"This isn't a good idea," I whisper, but I'm too far gone. I wouldn't be able to stop him even if I wanted to.

His other hand goes to the other side of my neck, and my hands go to his waist, my fingers gripping him. "This is about the best idea I've had in a really long, long time," he says right before he pulls me to him and his lips crush mine. My tongue comes out to touch his, and with the touch of him, the feel of him, I'm lost. I'm lost in him; I'm lost in the kiss. We both are. My hand roams up his chest to wrap around his neck, and I moan into his mouth. He tries to move his head to the left when we both hear a car door close. We jump apart as if we just got caught. "Fuck," he says as I run to the bathroom to make sure I have everything in place.

When I come back out, Emma is sitting at the counter, eating a peanut butter sandwich. "Boy, were you right to stay home." I look over at Gabe, who is stirring the soup.

"Did you eat?" I ask her, picking up the knife to continue buttering the bread.

"Barely. We walked into the barn and my hay fever started acting up right away. So I hightailed it back home and I'm taking this water bottle." She picks up the bottle in her hand. "I'm calling it a night. My body aches." She walks up the stairs, and I turn around to look for a frying pan.

"Crystal," he whispers, and I shake my head no, "we are going to discuss this."

I look up the stairs again, then bend to grab the pan. "No, we just got caught up in the moment." Putting the bread in the pan, I add the cheese. "It can't happen again."

"Why?" I turn my head to look at him. "Why not?" I tilt my head, not sure I heard the right words. "I'm single; you're single."

"You're my boss." I open the drawer to take a spatula out. "It just can't happen." I don't have time to say anything else because the other girls come in all giggling and a little tipsy.

"This country air," Ava says, walking up the stairs, "I need to sleep."

Corrine and Olivia follow her up the stairs. "I'm so tired; my legs are fucking killing me."

I look up the stairs and listen to the doors slam. "Please," I whisper to him, "not here."

"I'll give you this, but when we get home …" he says, turning the stove off and pouring the soup into two bowls.

So we sit at the island eating tomato soup and grilled cheese, and I wouldn't want to be anywhere else.

Chapter Eighteen

Gabe

"Okay, everyone, drive safely," I say as I get behind my wheel. We all pull away from the log house. I have never felt more unease in my life. The kiss was wrong, so fucking wrong, yet I couldn't help but want more. Her standing next to me, her in my space put me on my last nerve, and let's not even discuss the fact that only a wall separated us last night. I stared at that white wall almost all night long, which was a mistake because the team bonding bullshit the next day kicked my ass.

I just couldn't fucking get anything to work for me. The girls kept swapping out on me, and I swear to god, I would kill one of the instructors; I just didn't know which one. By the time I get into town, it's almost noon, so I hit up Walker's place. When I knock on the door and get no answer, I take out the emergency key under the mat. Like no one is going to look there, right?

"Anyone home?" I yell, walking into the house. Seeing it empty and quiet, I go to Walker's room and find him still in bed. "It's almost fucking noon," I say from the doorway.

"I thought you were gone on your weekend retreat?" he asks me as he rolls off the bed and goes straight to the medicine cabinet.

I shake my head and laugh, then head to the kitchen to start the coffee. We sit down, and he tells me about his drunken walk with Hailey, the woman who is creeping under his skin. I'm almost tempted to tell him about Crystal, but what would I say? *We had a one-night stand before she started working for me.* No, not going to happen, plus I don't want him looking at her like that. I leave him to his hangover, telling him I'm going to meet him at Gram's for dinner.

Needing to clear my head, I go to the one place I know I'm going to shut down—the gym. I work out for four hours, and between running on the treadmill, lifting weights, and pushing my body till I think my muscles are going to snap, I still can't erase her from my brain. I dress in my jeans, dress shirt, and sweater and make my way over to my grandmother's house. When I arrive, I figure she must have invited half the fucking town. I walk in, saying hello to a couple of people who I know. I head out into the backyard, and I find I wasn't wrong. Looking around, I try to spot my parents, but instead, my eyes land on the girl who is fucking everywhere.

She's standing with her perfect ass in white fucking jeans. A long-sleeve knitted sweater or some sort of concoction that is almost to her neck but falls down in the back, leaving the back of her shoulders bare. She's standing next to Luigi, who owns D'amore pizza, laughing at something he is saying, and I roll my eyes as I make my way to the bar. I order a beer, then lean against it, looking around. Once he hands it to me, I finally see Brody and Darla.

"You survived," Brody says, hugging me and smacking my back. This guy is a fucking ox. I'm in good shape, but he hurt my fucking back.

"Very funny." I take a pull of my beer. "I will say that I officially hate fucking camping now." I shake my head. "Hate it."

"I'm sure it wasn't that bad," Darla says, laughing while I glare at her.

"You think of the worst possible thing that can happen"—I point at her—"then times that by two. I'm going to see if my parents are here," I tell them. Walking away, I head inside and find Gram.

"Hey there, pretty boy," she says, kissing me on the cheek. "How was camping?"

"Brody and Walker here?" I ask her. "Oh, I see them." I nod at her, seeing that Walker arrived with Mila, and his face gets tight when he sees the girl he is trying to run from. When I walk outside this time, I'm stopped by a couple of people, all asking about the fucking camping trip. Did someone take out a billboard?

Making my way to the buffet, I grab a plate at the same time as a tiny hand grabs the same plate, and without looking up, I know it's her. My body knows she's near, my cock half saluting her, my heart beating a touch higher. "Take it," I tell her, not saying anything else. I pile food on my plate, turning around to see where my cousins are sitting. I pull out a chair at their table, and Crystal takes the one next to me. I don't listen to half the conversation around me because I can't. I'm fully aware of the woman next to me. Our arms touch on the table, and I just stare at them, then when her leg touches mine, she crosses her other foot so she leans into me a little more. Someone mentions cake, and Hailey and Crystal both jump up to go to the dessert table.

"Why were they invited?" I look at them, then the table.

"I'm going to go out on a limb here," Darla says, "and say that someone has gotten under your skin." She points at me.

"Please." I roll my eyes.

"I don't know if you know this, but Crystal is the talk of the salon. Ever since Mrs. Peterson broke her hip and she took care of her, she is the highlight of everyone's talk."

"I'm the one who operated on her, not my nurse."

"Oh, someone is sensitive," Brody says as he takes a pull from his beer bottle.

"Fuck you." I throw down my napkin. "I'm out." I walk around the pool to the side of the house, and I'm almost to my truck when I see someone I went to high school with who just came back into town.

"You look so different," Felicia says from beside me after she kisses me on my cheek.

"I could say the same about you." I smile at her. "California agreed with you."

"I loved it out there, but it was time to come home. Finished Sowing my wild oats." She smiles.

"Well, no place better to raise a family than here."

"That is what I think, too. So, you joined the family practice?"

"Yeah." I nod my head. "It's where I want to be."

"Well, we should totally do dinner one day and catch up. Do you still have the same number?" she asks, taking her phone out to scroll and repeat the number she has saved under my contact.

"That's it." I smile at her as she leans in one more time to kiss me on my cheek. I wave to her, watching her walk away from me. Looking at where she is going, I see Brody, Darla, and Crystal heading my way.

"You're still here?" Brody asks.

"Yes, I was just leaving." I look at them.

"Us, too. We have to drive Crystal home. Hailey isn't ready to go yet," Darla says.

"I'll take her. It's on my way," I say before I catch myself.

"Perfect," Brody says. We turn and walk toward the driveway. She walks toward my truck, stopping to hug Darla, and kiss Brody goodbye.

She turns to look at me. "You didn't have to drive me. I'll go back and get Hailey." She turns around, walking to the backyard.

I reach out to grab and stop her. "Get in the truck," I say through clenched teeth. This must be what they mean when they say breathing fire.

She pulls her hand free. "What's your problem?" She folds her arms, looking at me.

"My problem is that I had a rough couple of days," I tell her, leading her to the truck. I open the door for her. "I fucking hate camping." I push her in as she tries to hide the smirk.

"I knew you didn't like camping, but why did you suck at every single activity?" She turns and smiles at me. I step back, closing the door in her face. I march— yes, you read that right—I march to the driver's side and climb in.

"Buckle up," I tell her. Starting the truck, I buckle myself in.

"I get you're pissed because you sucked at every single activity, and that if push came to shove, you would be the one voted off the island first, but you shouldn't be that angry."

I turn right instead of turning left. I have no idea what I'm doing. "It wasn't because I didn't do well in the activities. It's…" I stop talking and look over at her. She's fucking beautiful, stunning; she is hands down the most beautiful person I have ever met, and her beauty goes deep. She isn't just a pretty face and a hot body; she has brains and compassion. That is when she doesn't make me want to bang my head against the wall, which is fifty percent of the time. "It's your fucking fault," I roar out, causing her to gasp in shock.

"My fault?" She puts her hands on her chest, her face shocked. "My fault? Why in the hell is any of this my fault?"

"You brought us up there for team fucking building," I say, going through the street that leads to my house. "Team bonding, my ass. I would have fired you all," I tell her as she pffts out and rolls her eyes. "Then you kiss me."

"What?" she yells, slapping her legs with her hands and then bringing them up. "I kissed you?" Her eyebrows pinch together. "You fucking kissed me." She points at me. "Getting all up in my space, breathing on me." I pull up to my house, thinking for once, *thank god it's so secluded.* "Coming all at me." She continues her rant, not even realizing we are parked. "You have some nerve with this whole 'you kissed me' bullshit."

"So you didn't kiss me back?" I ask her with my back to the door. She opens and then closes her mouth. "You didn't rake your fingers up my chest so hard I had red marks long after?" She glares at me. "You didn't moan into my mouth when I deepened the kiss?" I unbuckle my belt. "You didn't want more?"

She glares at me. "Nope." And rolls her lips together, putting her back against the truck door. I reach over, unbuckling her seat belt. "What?" she says in a whisper. She looks confused, not sure what is going on. Now she looks straight ahead and sees that we are parked. When I reach over and grab her to pull her to me, she comes willingly.

"Are you saying that if I kissed you again right now, you wouldn't want it?" I push my seat back with one hand, still holding her with the other. "Are you saying that if I kissed you right this minute, you wouldn't kiss me back, you wouldn't want it?" I pull her closer, thanking fuck I have a big ass truck with so much space. "Are you telling me that you didn't want me as bad as I wanted you?" My hands go to her hips, pulling her over to straddle my lap, her knees bent beside my hips. "Are you telling me I'm the only one who stayed awake all night long, thinking about sneaking into your room just to get a taste?"

"No," she whispers. This time, she makes the move, bending down and stopping just before she kisses my lips. "I don't know what it is." I don't let her finish. I slam my lips to hers, the kiss frantic. My lips on hers, her tongue with mine, our hands all over the place. My hands glide up her sides to cups her tits, squeezing them in my hands.

Her mouth leaves mine, and when she throws her head back and moans, I attack her neck. I bite and suck and kiss all at the same time. Her hands go under my sweater and shirt, but stop when I push her back against the steering wheel. Her shirt has shifted and now dips in the front, baring her shoulders. Pulling down the front, I hiss when I see her in a totally see-through strapless lace bra. Her nipples pink and pebbled, I lean down and bite one hard enough to hear her moan out loud while her hip moves up and down on my straining cock. "Oh my god." My eyes look up at her when I move to the other breast, doing the same thing with that nipple. "Why?" she asks the question, but I don't bother to answer her. I snap her bra off to bare her tits to me. Her hips ride me, trying to get more.

Feeling like a teenager making out in my fucking truck instead of grabbing her and bringing her to my bed, I suck a nipple into my mouth as her hands fly to my head. Her panting becomes louder and louder. I kiss my way over to the other one, sucking in her flesh before taking the nipple into my mouth. "Gabe," she whispers, looking down at me and pulling me up to her lips. She sits up, pressing my back to the seat, and my hands going to her ass. Grabbing her and pushing her into me, I feel her heat through both our jeans. Her mouth on mine, her tongue in my mouth. She goes right to left, trying to kiss me deeper. My hands at the nape of her neck pull her head back so I can kiss her neck, the neck that called out for me all night. I'm about to bite it when I hear a phone ringing.

"Shit," she says, snapping out of it. "That's mine." She leans over to get her purse and pulls out her phone. "Hey," she says into the phone. "Are you on your way?" She climbs off my lap, pushing her shirt up. "Yeah, I'm home. I'm going to bed, so I'll talk to you tomorrow." She tosses the phone down, looking at me. "Hailey is on her way home. How fast can you get me there?"

"What?" I look at her in confusion while she situates her sweater.

"If I'm not home when she gets there, and then I walk in after her, we are going to have to explain where the hell we were this whole time."

"So?"

"So?" She looks at me, buckling in. "So we can't tell anyone. How is it going to look if you're banging your new nurse?" I put my seat back and start the truck. "I think this thing is …" And she stops.

"What is this thing?" I ask her, driving faster than I normally do to get her home on time.

"We have an itch, and we need to scratch it." She smiles at me. "I mean, we are definitely attracted to each other, and the sex was decent the last time."

I glare over at her. "Decent, my ass. I rocked your world."

"Whatever." She rolls her eyes when I turn on her street. I pull up to see that Hailey's car isn't there yet. "Perfect," she says. Unbuckling and turning to look around, she leans over. "Okay, fine, it was a little better than decent." She kisses me on my lips and then jumps out of the truck, running up the steps. I watch her make it inside, then turn and drive back home, replaying what the fuck just happened.

"I almost had sex in my truck," I tell no one. "I would have totally fucked her in my truck, and I've never fucked in my truck."

I pull up to my house again. This time, when I open the door, her white bra falls at my feet. I bend to pick it up. "Decent, my fucking ass." I smile, walking up the step with her bra in hand. One day she is going to get this back, and I plan to make that day sooner than later.

Chapter Nineteen

Crystal

I rush up the stairs, my tits bouncing away with no bra. My heart beating so fast I don't think I can breathe. "What the fuck was all that?" I slam my bedroom door and lean against it as my chest rises and falls. My nipples sensitive from the friction of the knitted sweater. Pulling it over my head, I walk to my dresser to grab a tank top. Looking down, I see a hickey bright as day right next to my nipple. "Asshole."

I peel my jeans off my legs and toss them into the laundry basket. I put on a pair of shorts just as the front door opens and shuts. "Just in the nick of time," I say when I hear Hailey moving around downstairs. I open my Facebook app, wondering what my friends are doing back home, when I see I have a couple of friend requests. Darla, Emma, and Ava. I accept their requests and then see that Ava posted some pictures of this weekend. I click on her pictures going left to right when I see a picture of

Emma, Ava, Olivia, Mia, Corrine, and two other people I don't know with the caption "work squad." I click on the faces to see if they have been tagged. I notice one is Laura, the nurse I replaced, so I click on her face to take me to her Facebook page. She is private, but I see she has her work information entered, showing her new position at Chicago Memorial. I go back to Ava's picture and click on the other face, who is Bethany.

When I get to her Facebook page, her profile picture looks like it's from a yearbook. I swipe right, and my heart stops; there is Gabe and this woman taking a selfie. He kisses her neck while she smiles at the camera, showing off her engagement ring. The title is "I'm getting married," and I feel sick to my stomach. I sit up in bed going through the comments. They are all well wishes. Then I see a comment from Gabriel Walker.

Thank you for the wishes, so glad she said yes. I click on his name, and it takes me to his profile page, which is set to private. His profile picture is of him, Walker, and Brody standing around with beers in their hands. It is the only picture I could see. I try to click to see his friends, but it only shows me how many we have in common, which is two—Emma and Ava.

I taunt myself by going back and looking at the picture of him and the woman and then scrolling to find more pictures of them together. She is almost as tall as he is, and she is perfectly dressed every single time. Her hair and makeup done perfectly, she looks like she has a glam squad following her. On each picture, my eyes focus on Gabe's eyes; I can't point out anything, but he looks different. His eyes don't crinkle when he laughs. His smile is almost like it's for show. I go on Instagram and search to see if he has an account, and I can't find one, but I do find Bethany's and it's set to private.

I turn off my phone and shut down the lights, curling up in a ball to look at the blinking stars outside. I don't know how long I watch them before my eyes become heavy, and I fall asleep. I dream of Gabe and that little girl again, her eyes turning to look at me, but this time, my eyes are looking back at me as she smiles at me and waves.

My eyes flip open, the tears pouring out on the sides. I see it's light outside, the tears nonstop as I curl into a ball gazing outside. The sob comes out, my hand going to my mouth to muffle any noise. I've made my peace with never having a child, or at least I thought I did. My chest hurts, my heart aches. It's a physical pain I can't explain. A burning sensation, traveling from my chest to my stomach. When my alarm rings, my hand shoots out to shut it off. I slowly get out of bed, then wash my face with cold water, my eyes still a little puffy.

I go downstairs, doing my own routine, and leave without talking to Hailey. I walk in, keeping my head down, hoping like fuck my eyes look normal. "Morning," I tell Emma when I see her in the room, and she looks up at me and smiles.

"How excited were you to sleep in your own bed last night?" she asks, and I laugh.

"I about fucked my bed like a starfish." I wink at her while she laughs out loud. "Do you think I could start working with Dr. Walker Sr.?" I ask her, slipping on my Crocs. "Just so I know how he works."

"That sounds like a great idea," she says while we both walk to the nurses' station where everyone is standing around. "Crystal will be working with Dr. Walker Sr. today so she can get a feel for how he works."

"That's a negative." I hear from behind me. Turning, I see Gabe. "He's away till Wednesday, so I need to cover both patients for the day. It's going to be a busy day, ladies."

We all look up at the board to see that patients are scheduled every fifteen minutes for both doctors. "We are going to be here all night," Ava says.

"What can make it go faster," I start saying, "is for the nurses to go in first and assess the cases, so when Dr. Walker comes in, the nurses can give him the gist, more or less."

"That sounds like a good idea," Mia says. "We can maybe knock out the patient in five minutes instead of seven."

Everyone agrees on the plan. "See? Team building." I turn to smile at Gabe who glares at me. The buzzing tells us that a patient is in. "I'll take the first one."

And one by one, we roll for the day, and by the time five o'clock rolls around, my feet ache from practically running all day. I'm thankful for the two days of rushing around to keep my mind off my dream and prevent me from actually sitting down and talking to Gabe.

By the second day, I walk in, grabbing a piece of pie and going upstairs to collapse on my bed. I get up after a while and look outside to see Hailey sitting on the beach, but she isn't alone. No, this time Walker is there with her. I turn to take a shower, and when I get out, they are still together.

My stomach grumbles, so I go down to make something to eat. I listen to the back door open, going toward it.

"Late night visitor?" I say from the doorway. Hailey's back is to me, and she yelps.

"You scared the shit out of me," she tells me as I smirk at her.

"So … your visitor?" I ask her.

"You want to do this? What about the hickey on your left boob?" She points at me as my eyes go to slits.

"I don't know what you're talking about." I roll my eyes.

"Really? So who is the guy?" she asks me, and I just shrug my shoulders.

"Again, you're changing the subject." I point at her.

"So are you," she tells me when I turn to walk away, flipping her the bird. "Night, hooker." I walk upstairs to her laughter. I tried hard to hide the fucking hickey that has yet to fade, but when she walked into the bathroom yesterday while I was getting out of the shower, it was hard. I pick up my phone when I see I have a friend request, this time from Corrine. I accept it, then browse her Facebook page to see what she has on there. Pictures from the camping trip this weekend are at the top of her page.

I see she tagged me in one of the pictures, the one

with me and Gabe tied together at the wrist. My eyes glare at him as he tried to get me to go his way instead of the right way. The caption was "When Crystal wanted to kill Dr. Walker," and she tagged him.

I laugh at the picture but don't comment on it. When I walk in the next day, I see that Dr. Walker Sr. is back.

"We should go bowling," Olivia says. "Now, that is team bonding."

"I love bowling," Emma says.

"I want to go bowling," Ava says next.

"Oh, Dr. Walker, we are planning a bowling night," Corrine tells him when he comes to the nurses' station.

"Bowling, I can do," he says, and we all roll our eyes. "I can."

"Good morning, everyone." Dr. Walker Sr. walks in. "I saw the pictures from the retreat, and it looked like a great time. We have some news. We will be adding a pediatrician to the roster. Dr. Alan Holmes will be joining us. He will be here on Thursday."

The buzzer tells us that our first patient arrived, so we all get up. "Crystal, you're with me today." He smiles at me. "Let's see what all the fuss is about," he jokes, and I nod, making sure I am on my game today.

We work side by side the whole day with him asking my opinion and nodding when I'm right, which is ninety percent of the time. The other ten, when he explains why I was wrong, he does it with patience and kindness. When I finally leave that night, it's with a big old smile.

I get home, and Hailey is in the kitchen making pasta. "I had the best day at work," I tell her, sitting down at the table.

"Really?" she says, stirring the pasta. "I have to say I was nervous when you moved out here with me. I thought for sure you would hate it and leave me."

I smile. "Nah, but I am surprised I'm not bored." I grab an apple from the fruit bowl. "Today, I worked with Dr. Walker Sr., and I actually learned stuff. It was a great day."

"That's great."

"We are going bowling on Friday. I told them I was bringing my plus one." I wiggle my eyebrows at her. "It'll be fun."

"But I won't know anyone, and it's going to be weird. You guys will have your code words, and I'll be sitting there like a loner."

"We don't have code words, idiot." I shake my head when she places a plate in front of me. "Besides, you need to go out and have fun."

"Okay, fine," she says when she sits down, "but the minute I feel weird, I'm leaving."

"I promise you that I will make sure you don't feel weird." During the rest of the dinner, we discuss our plans this weekend about maybe going into town. When I get to work the next day, I see that I'm working with Dr. Walker Sr.

"I get it now," he says to me when I'm filling out a chart after the patient leaves. "Why everyone loves working with you."

I smile at him, turning my head back again. "Thank you. It means a lot coming from you," I tell him, and we go back to work. The next day I come in and I'm excited to be working with Mrs. Dr. Walker.

"I'm excited," she says, walking into the examine room. "My husband has done nothing but brag about you this whole week."

I laugh because he has been openly telling all his patients about me.

I work side by side with her all day. She very much has a soft approach to all her patients, who are mainly women. "You really have a touch with patients," she says, washing her hands after her patient leaves. "Mrs. Naya hates every single one of the nurses here. Refuses to even talk to them, but you." She shakes her hands, grabbing a paper towel. "You buttered her up and she told you her whole life story."

"It's nothing," I tell her.

"It's something." She leans her hip to the counter. "When Laura and Bethany left, this place was meek and dire. It was like we lived under a dark cloud, ready to pour down on us. Lightning and thunder," she says. "Now it's like a ray of sunshine, people are smiling, well, not Gabe, he's been touchy this week."

I try not to change my facial expression when she mentions Gabe. "None of the nurses will he fight for, but low and behold, he called his father last night demanding to work with you today."

I shake my head. "I don't know."

She smiles. "He just knows good when he sees it." She turns to walk out of the room, leaving that lingering in the air.

The week flies by, and by the time I look around, we are getting in the Uber to go to the bowling alley. "You look awesome," I tell Hailey.

"It feels good to dress up," she says, looking over at me.

"Yeah, feels nice not to have my scrubs on," I say, looking down at my skintight blue jeans with rips in the front and a long-sleeve black bodysuit with a round criss-cross neckline. My hair loose and wavy. "I'm planning to let loose tonight." I wink at her as I put on my pink lip-gloss.

"Here we are," the driver says, and we get out of the car. We both plan on drinking tonight so we decided to Uber it. Walking in, I look around and see a couple of the people have arrived. I introduce Hailey to Emma and Mia, who quickly start talking. I look up to see Gabe staring at me or, better yet, glaring at me.

I give him a chin up when he motions with his head for me to follow him. I walk away from the girls who are talking about some recipe and follow Gabe out the side entrance. "What's the matter?" I ask, crossing my arms over my chest.

He looks around and then grabs my hand, dragging me with him around a corner to an alley. It's a dead-end alley with two dumpsters. "What the hell?" I ask him. I'm about to say more when I'm pushed to the wall next to the dumpster. "Gabe," I whisper to him when he comes to stand in front of me, his eyes a dark blue.

"You've been avoiding me." My back is against a cold brick wall, my legs opened a bit where he's stepped between them. "All week, I've tried to get some time with you, and you just avoided everything." I finally take in his outfit; he looks like he can be on the cover of *GQ*. His light blue jeans ripped at the knee, a dark blue jean shirt buttoned up the front. The cuffs turned and rolled up, showing off his ink and I get the need to trace it with my fingers or better yet my tongue. White running shoes on his feet.

"I have not been avoiding you." I try to settle my erratic heartbeat.

He looks in my eyes, and then down at my chest, his forefinger tracing the edges around my breast. "All week, I wanted to talk to you."

"Really?" I laugh. "About the fact you gave me a hickey?"

His head flies up. "I did not."

"Oh"—my hand grasps my top, and I move it down an inch to show him the now fading hickey—"you most certainly did."

His finger reaches out to touch it, and he chuckles. "I guess I did."

"Yeah, well …" His mouth shuts me up. Fuck, can he kiss. He can kiss better than anyone I have ever kissed. His tongue invades me, his hands on my hips now. He kisses me, leaving me breathless and senseless. I can't think when he's kissing me.

"I think I need to return the favor," I finally say when he leaves my lips to kiss down my neck. I unbutton his shirt until it gapes open. My hand touches his hot skin, and he hisses. "I forgot what you looked like," I say when my finger runs down his chest. I lean in, biting his nipple and then sucking right next to it, exactly where he gave me a hickey. I look up and see him watching me, but he doesn't give me a second more. Instead, he pushes me back against the wall and attacks me with his mouth. We moan into each other's mouths, my leg lifting over his hip, making it the perfect position for him to slide into me if we weren't wearing pants.

"Tonight," he says when he leaves my lips. "Don't give a fuck how pissed you are or how much you avoid me. Tonight, you're coming home with me, and we are going to fuck each other out of our systems." He rolls his hips, the friction hitting my clit. "Tell me you get me."

I nod. "That is what we need to do. One more time just to get it out of our system." I lean forward, kissing him when I bite his lower lip. "One night, like the last time."

"Deal," he says, and I push off the wall.

"Don't follow me in," I say over my shoulder. "Wait a couple of minutes." I walk to the front, going in the door.

"There you are." I hear Hailey say from beside Walker.

"Sorry, I forgot something in the car," I say, avoiding eye contact with her while I grab my shoes.

Hailey laughs next to me. "That's funny. We didn't bring my car here."

My head snaps up. Fuck. "Did we pick teams already?" I ask, walking away and praying to fuck that no one else noticed I was gone.

Chapter Twenty

Gabe

I watch her walk away from me, swinging her hips, and I make a whole list of fucking things I'm going to do with that ass tonight. This is the best idea I've had ever. We just need one more night to fuck off these frustrations. I've been on edge since I attacked her in my truck. Every single day, I've tried to get a minute with her, but it's been so busy we haven't had the time. I came so close to showing up at her house, but I didn't know if she had told her cousin. I look back at my chest and see the little hickey she gave me; it's not as good as the one I gave her. I didn't even know I had given her one, but seeing my mark on her almost made me want to beat my fist on my chest.

I walk in, rubbing the lip-gloss off my lips with my thumb, when I see Walker look at me with his eyebrows pushed together. I have no idea what is going on, but Hailey is beside him, and when she sees me walking in, her eyes go big and her mouth opens. Walker leaves her and meets me halfway.

"You are fucking Crystal? Are you insane?" he hisses.

"Hey," I say, pointing at him, "I'm not fucking any-one." And at that exact moment, it's the truth. I'm not fucking anyone, but tonight ... tonight, I'm going to be fucking her.

"Really?" He tilts his head, looking at me. "You still have lip-gloss on your lips, and your shirt is not buttoned properly."

"Fuck," I say, turning and walking to the bathroom. I walk inside and see that I have lip-gloss all over my fucking face. I grab some brown paper towels, wet them, and wipe it off. When I walk back out, I see that Brody, Darla, Walker, and Hailey are all together. "So did you guys make the teams?" I ask, avoiding anyone's eyes.

"We did," Walker says. "It's going to be six of us. Against six of them." He points at the other side. I see Crystal standing with the other nurses socializing.

"So," Walker says, sitting next to Hailey. "Who is go-ing to go first?"

Darla jumps to her feet. "I'll go first," she says as she gives Brody a kiss. I watch her walk down the lane, and her ball knocks down four pins. Shaking my head, I grab a beer from the tray next to Brody.

"Hailey," Brody says loudly, and I turn seeing her jump away from Walker. "Your turn."

Going to the balls, she grabs a pink ball and looks over at Alan in the other lane. They discuss something, and she watches him bowl, then repeats what he did and knocks down eight pins. She squeals and then walks back over and high-fives him.

"Who the fuck is that?" Walker asks from beside me.

"Don't fucking touch my pediatrician. He just started. He's the best around." I look over to see Crystal talking to a guy I don't recognize. Walker jumps out of his chair and goes to introduce himself while I laugh to myself.

Crystal finally comes over to sit beside me. "When is it my turn?" she asks, looking up at the board. "I'm after Walker."

"Yeah. But I can say with confidence that I'm going to win tonight."

She folds her arms over her chest. "Really?" And she laughs. "Is that a fact?"

"It is." I take a sip of beer then hand it to her. She grabs the plastic cup of beer, taking a sip. "We should bet."

"Oh, really?" she says right when Walker finishes, and it's her turn. She looks around and then leans in. "How about if you lose, you give head first." She whips herself out of her chair. "Is that a deal?" she says over her shoulder.

"What is a deal?" Darla asks, looking at us.

"Winner buys the other one lunch for a week," I say to her as Crystal picks up her ball. "No way she can win. Her shot is going to be soft."

I see Crystal line up and then walk out, throwing the ball straight down the middle. I close my eyes before the ball touches the pins, saying a silent prayer, but it isn't answered. Instead, I hear her fucking squeal.

"Soft, my ass," she says as she comes back and sits next to me. "I believe it's your turn. Loser buys the winner lunch for a week." She smiles at me while I glare at her. "Should I just give you my orders now?"

"It isn't over till the tenth frame, doll face," I tell her, picking up a ball.

"Aww, did you just call me doll face?" Her face scrunches in a grimace. "I mean, it's better than pain in my ass." She shrugs.

"You are a pain in my ass. For once, I'd like to have a day when you don't second-guess everything I do," I say, lining up my ball while she yells.

"For once, I'd like to go to work with a doctor who I don't have to second-guess. If you want, I can transfer to pediatrics. Alan likes me," she tells me, egging me on as she leans back and smiles at Alan, who waves. I look at the ball, contemplating throwing it at Alan's face. "Let's see what you can do, Doctor," Crystal says as I bowl, throwing the ball harder than I wanted to, but it goes straight down the middle and knocks down all the pins. I turn around with my hands over my head.

"You two do realize that this is ten frames, and we just did only one?" Brody says as he grabs Darla to sit on his lap.

"Please. I got him beat; he's a princess," Crystal says as she gulps down some beer.

"Princess?" I laugh at her. "You cried when I picked up a frog and showed it to you."

Crystal slams down her hands. "That fucker was going to jump at me." She storms up. "I want to change teams."

Everyone laughs at us. "Too late," I tell her, looking up at the screen. "Darla, you're up."

We watch Brody and Darla take their turn and turn to see Walker and Hailey with their heads together. "You think they are going to bang tonight or another night?" I ask her when she shakes her head.

"It's safe to say, between the two of you, you're the only one getting banged tonight." She laughs, drinking more beer.

"Hooker," Crystal yells, and Hailey jumps up. "You're up."

For nine frames, we one-up each other. Until the eighth round. I'm about to go, and I just bowled a strike, so if I knock a spare, I'll blow her out of the water. She knows that, and she leans in when she comes over and sits after her turn. "Your turn." I get up to get my ball and she follows me. "And just so you know…" She turns and sees that everyone else is talking and not paying attention while I grab my ball. "I played with myself all week thinking about you." My hand grips the ball, and I'm pretty sure if it was glass, it would shatter. "I even did it right before we got here." She smiles and then walks away. I close my eyes, trying to keep the blood from flowing to my cock, who is trying to get out. I open my eyes, throwing the ball down the lane with so much force it goes left and knocks down only two pins. What a waste of a shot. I'm in a daze the rest of the game, not even sure I can talk to someone without cracking. Brody ends up winning the game, and Crystal beats me by one point.

"The machine is broken," I say, looking down at the score sheet. "There must be a glitch in the system. I had one more strike than you did."

Crystal looks at her nails and then up again. "Yes, and then you knocked two pins down, which means you suck and I win, so ... I'll text you my orders."

I don't have time to say anything else because the rest of the staff comes over and discusses hitting up the bar. Crystal looks at Hailey. "You go ahead. I'm going to head home," she says as she looks around.

"Walker"—Crystal shouts—"you going home? Can you drive her?"

"I'm not going to the bar," Alan says with a smile. I swear I see steam coming from Walker's ears as he steps in and leads Hailey away.

"Okay, so we are going to the pub?" Crystal says. "Can I catch a ride with you?" I nod my head.

"Anyone else need a ride?" But everyone is already on their own. Once we get in the truck, I turn to look at her. "I'm not wasting time at this fucking bar. We make an appearance for ten minutes, and then we leave."

"We can't leave together," she tells me. "That's too obvious."

"Fine," I hiss and I text her my address. I pull my house key from my keys. "You leave first, and then I'll follow you."

"Ohh, alone in your house?" She smiles, getting out and putting the key away. "What am I going to do with all that spare time?" she asks right before I pull open the door.

"You can get naked in my bed and play with yourself until I get there." She stops in her tracks, looking around. "Besides, I lost, so I give head first. Gotta say, I was hoping to lose." I wink at her as she groans.

"Five minutes," she hisses. "I'm suddenly not feeling well."

I throw my head back and laugh as I join the rest of the staff. Crystal takes off to shoot pool while Ava corners me. "So this was fun, right?" she says, leaning into me. "I'm glad we did it. It's always fun to get out of the office and let loose."

"Yeah, it is." I smile at her and see she has gotten a touch closer. "But I'm not feeling so well. I think I might hit the road."

"Really?" She pouts. "That's too bad." She touches my arm and walks away. I catch Crystal's gaze, nodding. She looks around and then says goodbye to everyone with the excuse she is exhausted. I wave goodbye to her as I watch her leave. She texts me two minutes later.

In the Uber.

I text her back.

On my way!

I walk around, saying goodbye to everyone and wishing them a good weekend. I walk out to my truck and see that my tires have been slashed. "What the fuck is this?" I say, looking around to see if anyone is there, but no one is around. "This can't be fucking happening." I walk around the truck; all four tires are fucking finished. I pick up my phone, calling Crystal first.

"Hello."

"Hey, I'm stuck," I tell her. "Someone slashed my tires."

"Shut up," she says. "If you didn't want to have sex with me, you could have just said no. You didn't have to slash your tires." She laughs. "Do you want me to go home?"

"Your ass had better be naked on my bed when I get there." I hang up on her and call Walker, who sounds just as thrilled as I am.

"This had better be you dying."

"It's one step from death," I tell him. "Someone slashed my fucking tires, and I really need a ride home. Like really, really." I'm even to the point I might even fucking beg him.

"Yeah, yeah, I'm on my way," he says as he hangs up the phone.

Just then a text comes through from Crystal.

I have arrived.

I put my head back, counting down the fucking minutes.

I'm in your room.

Is that my bra?

I laugh when she sends me a selfie of herself holding the bra, and I see my headboard in the background.

Why are you not naked?

Who says I'm not.

It's followed up with a picture of her bare legs on my comforter. My cock gets so hard he might combust. I see Walker's truck pull into the parking lot. I don't even wait for him to stop before jumping in. "I will pay whatever ticket you get, but you have to get me home."

He throws his head back and laughs while Crystal sends me another picture of her hip, and I can see black lace. I grip the phone in my hand, tapping my foot. I jump out of the truck when we make it to my house. "Leave." I slam the door and run inside. Closing the door, I take the steps two at a time, but nothing could have prepared me for what I saw.

There in the middle of my king-size bed on my white comforter is Crystal.

Her black bra is pushed down under her tits, her nipples peaked and pebbled, her back against the pillow. Her legs are bent at her knees but open to show me that beneath the black lace thong, her fingers are playing with herself. "Took you long enough," she moans and comes on her fingers while I watch her.

"Playtime is over," I tell her, getting closer to the bed. "For you, that is. I'm just starting." Her eyes watch me.

Chapter Twenty-One

Crystal

"Playtime is over." His voice comes out gruff, strong, and my body gets tense again.

He told me naked on his bed. I gave in halfway.

He unbuttons his shirt button first. "You listened." His shirt falls open, and I stare at his big, strong chest, my eyes flying to the mark I made on his chest in that alley.

When the driver pulled up to his house, my hands were sweaty, and I had to wipe the palms on my pants. I unlocked the door, looking around at the big, open house. I walked up the stairs in his huge house, coming to his bedroom. I flipped on the light, taking in the huge bedroom. Brown wood beams are across the ceiling. Two gray chairs beside the windows on the side of a big king-size bed. I drop my purse in one of them, kicking off my shoes. I peel off my jeans, folding them, and then unsnap the bodysuit and pull it over my head. I walk to the king-size bed with the gray headboard. I climb on and sink down; it's almost like a cloud. With his smell all around me, I did what he told me to do. I got ready for him. Now he's here in front of me, peeling off his shirt. I thought I had his chest memorized in my head, but I was fucking wrong. Because there is no way those memories did him justice.

His hands go to the top button of his jeans, kicking off his shoes while he pulls the zipper down. His black boxers hide what he has underneath. He pulls his pants off, leaving them in a heap at his feet. He climbs onto the bed, his hands pushing my knees to the sides so I open more to him. He pulls my one hand out of my panties and brings my fingers to his mouth. "Thanks for keeping her warm," he says, sucking the juices off my fingers.

The hand that was holding mine now rubs down the length of my lace-covered slit. "How fond are you of these panties?" he asks. But he doesn't wait for an answer because he rips them off me, the lace no match to his strength, and then he tosses them to his bedside table where I found my bra. "To add to the collection." He winks at me, and my stomach sinks. He looks down now, and I'm open for him. "Time for me to pay my debts." He smiles, getting on his stomach with his arms beside my hips.

I watch him blow on my wet slit, his mouth so close I tilt my hips up, and he licks from the bottom to the top, sucking on my pussy. My head flies back as I take in the warmth of his mouth. His hands push my legs back while he licks me up and down, his tongue circling my clit. "Fuck," I pant out.

My hands go to his head as his licks get harder, and he teases me more. He looks up, watching me, now biting my clit when he gets there and then licking back down. "Do that again," I beg him. And I see him smirk as he does it again. My hands go back to the headboard as I try to ride his face. I'm frantic with need; I need him to just give it to me. His hands move up to my tits, rolling my nipples while he bites my clit. I move my hips side to side, and he still doesn't give it to me. I groan in frustration, one of my hands squeezing the pillow while the other hand goes to his head. I hold his head as I try to move. His hands let go of my tits, sliding down, and he puts one finger in me, then two. I thrust my hips to meet his fingers as he sucks my clit into his mouth, and I close my eyes and fly off the cliff, coming on his fingers so hard.

I lie back on his pillow, my chest rising and falling fast. My breathing trying to get back to normal. He leans over, opening his nightstand drawer to take out a condom. I watch him sheath himself, taking his cock in his hand and positioning it at my opening. I'm waiting, now almost holding my breath for him to enter me. We both moan as he slides into me a bit at a time till he's buried fully inside me. "Definitely not what I remembered," I tell him with my palm on his stomach as he slides in and out. We watch each other the whole time, never once looking away, except when we both come and our eyes close at the same time.

We spend the night savoring every single second. I thought the hotel room was the best sex I had, but I lied.

This, right here, tonight, which turned into early morning, is the best sex I've had in my life.

We are on his couch, after coming down to get something to drink and eat, and I straddle his lap with his cock buried in me. I collapse on top of him, my eyes growing heavy. He places me on my side, sliding out of me to go take care of the condom. "You want to go back to my room?" he asks, and I just nod my head, or at least I think I'm nodding my head. Who knows at this point. My body is limp, and I'm curled up naked on the couch when I hear him laugh. He picks me up off the couch and carries me up the stairs, placing me in his bed that must be the definition of heaven. I turn on my side, feeling him slide in behind me and pull the covers over us. I close my eyes, telling myself I'm just going to take a power nap and then head home.

I don't know how long I sleep or even what time it is, but when I get up, I walk to the bathroom. Finishing up, I grab my clothes to get dressed while I watch him sleep. When I'm fully dressed, I go back to the bed. I lean down to kiss him as he groans. "I'm leaving," I whisper, knowing he isn't going to hear me. I sneak out of the house when I see my Uber pull up. I climb in the car, my muscles screaming at me, and close my eyes.

"We've arrived." I hear the Uber driver say. I thank him and walk into the house, hoping I can sneak in, but no luck. Hailey is walking into the kitchen when I get in.

"Did you leave to go out for doughnuts, or is this your walk of shame?" she asks me as she walks to the machine and starts the coffee.

"I don't want to discuss it." I walk to the table and pull out a chair. I place my head on the table, my phone buzzing in my pocket. "I'm going to sleep till Monday."

I close my eyes while I hear her making coffee, the smell almost perking me up. "I kissed Jensen last night." I hear her say and lift my head from the table.

"With tongue?" I ask her as she nods her head like a badass. "HUSSY!" I yell, laughing and slapping the table. "And how was it?"

I see her struggle to put it into words, her mouth opening and closing a couple of times when she says just one word. "Perfect." She smiles. "Absolutely perfect."

"I thought he would knock the shit out of Alan and bowl with his head. Every single time." I laugh, grabbing one of the cups of coffee and taking a sip. "It was quite funny. Gabe and I had a side bet going."

"You and Gabe have a lot going," she counters, and I bend my head, not willing for her to see that I'm in over my head. Last night was supposed to get it out of our system, but I'm afraid it made it even worse. "I know you're a big girl, but I want you to be careful. I mean, he's your boss."

"Technically, his father is my boss, but it was a one-time thing." I point at her, and she glares at me. "Okay, fine, it was more than a one-time thing, but it's done." I put my hands up, not willing to tell her about the first time we were together. That's my secret. The only other secret I'm not sharing with her. "No blood, no foul, or whatever the country folks say."

"I think it's no harm, no foul, country or not," she

says, sitting up. "I just don't want you to get hurt."

"Hailey, it's fine." I look up and then down. "I promise I'm okay." I get up from the table, grabbing my cup of coffee and walking up the stairs while my phone continues to buzz in my purse. I close the door, then take my phone out of my purse.

"Hello."

"You just left," he says angrily.

"I told you I was leaving." It isn't a lie; I did. "And you mumbled something and turned over."

"I'm pretty sure if I had heard you say you were leaving, I wouldn't have let you leave," he says while I start to undress. "I swear to god, I'm going to cuff you to me next time," he says, and I hear rustling in the background.

"Well, too late. I'm home now, and I'm going to bed to sleep till Monday." I laugh. "You wore me out, and I don't think I can move."

He chuckles. "I have to get up and get my truck. Call me when you wake up."

I close my eyes, ignoring the feelings creeping into me. The butterflies starting to fluff their wings. "Gabe."

"Later, doll face," he says, hanging up.

"Why the fuck is he calling me doll face?" I shake my head and crawl under the covers, hating my bed all of a sudden. I don't know if it's so much that I hate my bed or that I love his more. "Ugh." I get back up to close the shades and make the room as dark as possible, then fall sound asleep. When I wake, it's still dark, or darker, I should say. Grabbing my phone, I see it's almost seven p.m. "Fuck, I actually slept the whole day." I get up and go downstairs, finding a note from Hailey on the counter.

Gone to have dinner at Jensen's. Be back later.

With a smile, I open the fridge and find nothing that I like or, better yet, nothing I can pop into the microwave. I groan, shutting the fridge door. I go upstairs and take a shower, which makes me feel a little bit more human and refreshed. I grab my phone and the truck keys. "Pizza," I say to myself, making my way to D'Amore. I park the truck, walking around the corner, and stop in my tracks. There in the middle of the sidewalk is Gabe with a blonde holding his hand. My stomach falls, my heart speeds up, and heat rises up to my neck.

"This was fun." I hear her giggle when she turns to look at him as he smiles at her. Asshole. "We need to do this again soon."

I don't stay around for him to answer. I walk back to my car with my head down. I put the key in and then reverse out of my parking space, trying to get out of here, but they walk right in front of my car. Gabe and the blonde as she still holds his arm with both his hands in his pocket. He sees me, and his face goes white, his mouth opens and closes as the blonde pulls him along with her. I turn, driving out of the parking lot, and make my way to the house. I close the front door and turn off all the lights, walking up to my room. Ten minutes go by when I hear a knocking at the door. "Crystal, open the door!" he shouts, and I brace myself, get up, and walk to the door, swinging it open.

"What is it?" I tell him, my hand holding the doorknob so hard I think it might snap off.

"Why did you just take off?" he says with his hands on his hips.

"Well, I went out for food, then I got sick to my stomach, so I came back home." I look around him. "Where did you leave your date?"

He glares at me. "I wasn't on a date."

"Whatever, doesn't really matter to me." I shrug. "Now, if you'll excuse me, I have a bath that is calling my name," I say and slam the door in his face. I hear him curse and then storm down the steps. I walk upstairs to my room and sit here in the dark with my back against my bedroom door. I look down at my phone, see that he is calling, and send him straight to voicemail. I crawl into bed, his name popping up on my phone.

Would you please let me explain?

Crystal

Please

I shut off my phone and place it on my bedside table. *It's for the best; it couldn't go anywhere anyway*, I tell myself. Except for the first time in my life, I'm sad that it's over. For the first time in my life, I let my walls down, and for the first time in my life, I cry for a boy.

Chapter Twenty-Two

Gabe

My feet drag against the sidewalk as I walk into D'Amore. I spent the whole fucking day fixing my truck and the four slashed tires. Cut straight through.

I rub my neck while I look around to see if someone can take my order for takeout. I look down at my phone to see if Crystal has texted me.

It's been all day, and nothing. No word. I'm giving her until nine, and then I'm going to her house. I don't give a fuck. I place my order with Luigi who comes over as I'm scrolling through my emails.

"Gabe." I hear from beside me and look over to see Felicia. "I thought that was you." She smiles, coming over and kissing my cheek.

"Are you here alone?" she asks me.

"Um, yeah, I'm picking up some pie for home," I tell her.

"So am I," she tells me, standing there. "Look at us

with our crazy Saturday night plans." I chuckle. "Are you in a rush?"

"Not really," I say the truth; I'm biding my time till I can go to Crystal's.

"Great," she says. "Let's sit and eat. I'm tired of eating by myself."

"Sure," I say, pointing at a table. "Luigi, I'm going to eat here," I tell him as he nods at me. Our pizzas arrive a couple of minutes later. We talk about her moving back, what she's missed since she's been gone, and we laugh about stories from when we graduated.

I get up to walk out, and she wraps her hand around my arm. I look down at her fingers, wanting to shake her hand away from me.

"This was fun," she says when we get to the sidewalk, and she faces me. "We need to do this again soon."

"Um. Felicia. I'm not ready to date anyone," I tell her, and she nods her head. "Just so we are clear."

She nods her head. "Crystal." The word makes my stomach flip. "I'm parked over there." She points behind her.

"So am I," I say. When we turn to walk to our vehicles, she grabs my arm again. I'm looking down, not paying attention, when a car pulls up while we are walking. Looking at the car, I feel my stomach that was flipping two seconds ago fall. As I take in Crystal's eyes watching us. I don't say anything because Felicia pulls me along. I turn to say something to Crystal, but she just rushes off.

"Sorry." I shake her hand from my arm. "I have to

go." I jog to my truck, pulling out and making my way to her house. "Fuck, fuck, fuck," I chant, pulling up to her house and seeing it pitch black. I rush up the steps and bang on the door. "Crystal, open the door!" I shout. I'm not sure she is going to answer the door, but she surprises me when she swings it open and I see her in her black yoga pants and a thick sweater. She's so beautiful.

"What is it?" she asks me, her hand holding the door.

"Why did you just take off?" I ask her, putting my hands on my hips.

"Well, I went out for food, then I got sick to my stomach, so I came back home," she says and then looks around my shoulder to the left and to the right. "Where did you leave your date?"

I glare at her. "I wasn't on a date."

"Whatever, doesn't really matter to me." She shrugs, and I have this incredible urge to pound my fist somewhere. "Now, if you'll excuse me, I have a bath that is calling my name." She slams the door in my face.

"Fuck." I throw my head back and rub my face with my hands. I turn, walking back to my truck, and slam the door so hard I'm surprised the windows didn't shatter. I drive back to my house, slamming the front door. "Un-fucking-believable," I say to the empty house. I pull out my phone to text her.

Would you please let me explain?
Crystal
Please

I stand in the kitchen, waiting for her to answer, waiting for something, but nothing comes through. I march up to my room, pulling off my clothes, and finally climb under the covers only for her smell to hit me right away. "Fuck," I groan when my cock wakes up, thinking she's near me. I toss and turn all night. The fact she's pissed at me bugs the living shit out of me. I get up and make my way to Walker's house; he'll know what to do. I pull up and see that Brody's truck is already there. When I open the door and walk in, I see Brody, Darla, Walker, and Hailey.

"What the fuck? Is this a meeting?" I ask, walking to the counter, opening the doughnut box, and taking one out. A knock on the back door has us all turning to see Crystal there looking in. "Fuck," I say as I bite into the doughnut again. Hailey walks over to the door and opens it.

"Seriously, you can't go out without your phone. I was texting you all night," she tells her as I start coughing. Funny, she didn't answer me all night.

"You spent the night?" I ask as I continue to choke on my doughnut. "I need water." I open the fridge and grab a beer instead. "Why are you here?" I point at Crystal.

"I was making sure she was okay. Why are you here?" She folds her arms over her chest, bringing her tits up on her chest.

"This is my cousin's house," I say, and I watch all four heads go from me to Crystal as they follow our conversation.

"Well, my cousin went out for dinner, and it's breakfast, so …" she says as she tosses her hair behind her shoulder, leaving her neck bare. A neck I want to bite.

"So you thought you would cock block her?" I smirk. "Nice."

"I wasn't cock blocking her; I was making sure she was okay. Why are you here? Did your date wake up and notice what an asshole you were?" I knew she was pissed about that.

"I told you, she wasn't a fucking date." I smash the can of beer in my hand.

"Whatever. I couldn't care less." She rolls her eyes at me, and I want to smash a wall.

"Okay." Walker claps his hands together. "Who wants breakfast? Darla?"

"I'm sorry." She blinks her eyes. "She spent the night?" She points at Hailey. "And Gabe wants Crystal?"

"I don't want her," I say at the same time Crystal yells, "Oh, he doesn't want me," and we glare at each other.

"I actually slept on the couch," Hailey says, "and nothing happened." I don't listen to anything that anyone is saying. Instead, I look at Crystal.

"Honey," Darla says to Brody. "I think we need to go outside and walk back inside," she whispers as he bends down to kiss her.

"I would love, love something to eat," Crystal says as she walks into the kitchen and grabs a doughnut. "I can make the toast." She chews on a piece of doughnut. "Hailey makes the best pancakes of life."

"I can make pancakes," Hailey says, wrapping her hands around Walker's waist.

"I can make the bacon," Brody says.

"I can set the table," Darla says.

"That means you can leave." Crystal looks at me. "You might have another date waiting." She smirks at me, and I grind my teeth.

"I'm not leaving." I cross my arms over my chest, and I've fucking had it. This is over. "Me and you are going to have words later," I tell her as she rolls her eyes at me.

"I don't have to speak to you before Monday," she says as she turns to face me, "so I guess we can talk then." I'm done with this. I walk to her, and when she looks up at me, I bend over and throw her over my shoulder. I'm going to make her fucking listen to me if it's the last thing I do.

"Now." I carry her outside to the backyard, but I don't go far because she starts screaming.

"You asshole. You're hurting me," she yells, and I stop and put her down. The horror that I actually hurt her makes it too much for me to breathe.

"Where are you hurt?" I ask, checking her out, as she slaps my hands away.

"You hurt my stomach," she says as she tries to shoo me away.

"I didn't mean to," I say softly, putting my hand on her stomach and she lets me. "Are you okay?"

"Yes," she says, walking away from me and back into the house.

"Are we going to eat or not?" she asks as she opens the fridge and takes out a water bottle.

No one says anything as I look at the sky, mumbling to myself, "What the fuck?" We all go into the kitchen and take our places to try to cook breakfast. The saying too many cooks in the kitchen is in fact the right one. With every turn, we are bumping into someone. We finally finish and all eat outside.

Brody and Darla are the first to leave, kissing us all goodbye, Darla smirking at me the whole time.

"Let's go," I tell Crystal when I stand. Enough with the stalling.

"No, thanks," she tells me as she turns and walks out the back door, slamming it on the way.

"That fucking woman is going to be the death of me," I say, turning and walking out the front door, slamming it. "Fine, she doesn't want to talk. I won't bother to explain myself," I say out loud. "Her loss." But I don't take one more step. Instead, I turn around, walk through the house again, and run out the back door, yelling her name.

I finally catch up to her on the beach. "Would you please give me a fucking second to explain?" I stop her from walking by standing in front of her with my hands on my knees as I try to catch my breath.

"Nothing to explain," she says, the wind making her hair fly all over the place as she tries to catch it in her hand.

"Really?" I say, standing up now. "So you're not pissed that you saw me with another woman?"

"Nope," she says, shaking her head. "I mean, if you saw me out with another man, you wouldn't care either, right?"

The thought of her on a date with another man has me flexing my hands into a fist. "It would piss me the fuck off."

She crosses her arms over her chest. "Really?" she says.

"Fucking really," I say, looking up at the sky and back down again. "Felicia and I went to school together, and she just moved back to town. I saw her at Gram's when she had the dinner and then again when I went for pizza," I say, walking closer to her. "I was out eating and waiting for your phone call. I was biding my time until you called me, or until nine, when I was just going to show up at your house," I tell her, tucking her flying hair behind her ear. "I wasn't on a date."

"It doesn't matter," she says, not giving in, but my hands go to her shoulders. "We said we wanted one more night, and we got it."

"What if I want another night, or two nights?" I ask her as she looks up at me. "What if we just continue doing what we are doing without a timeframe?"

"What the hell are you talking about?" she asks.

"I like you, when you don't drive me crazy," I tell her. "And I want you all the time, even when you drive me crazy." I smile at her and lean down to kiss her lips. "Sometimes more when you drive me crazy."

"This is a really bad idea," she says, but her hands go to my hips. "Like really bad. I don't want to be known as the whore of the clinic."

"We don't have to tell anyone, well except for the four people who already know." I raise my eyebrows. "And we can just take it one day at a time?"

"No hanky-panky at work," she tells me. "That is a fine line I refuse to cross. If at any point I feel you pushing it, I will cut you."

"Fine, no hanky-panky at work." I bring her closer. "Is the parking lot considered work?"

"Yes." She nods. "No kissing in public either."

"Trust me, the last thing I want to be is the talk of the town," I tell her. "I've had enough of that over the past couple of months."

"Okay. Also, no dating other people while we are together," she says, and I glare at her. "If we want to date someone else, we walk away."

"Yeah," I say. At this point, I would agree with whatever she wants just to get one more day with her.

Chapter Twenty-Three

Crystal

"You're way off base here," Gabe says to me. "I've known these two since high school." He's talking about the woman patient we just had who came in with a gash on her head that required five stitches.

I cross my arms over my chest. "I'm saying her story doesn't add up. How the fuck do you get a bump on your head from taking a cardboard box down?"

He puts his hand in his lab coat pocket. "I'm not saying it adds up; I'm just saying that I think you're off base."

"I think you aren't looking at this the right way," I counter with my back against the wall. It's been three weeks since we had that talk on the beach, three weeks of sneaking around, and let me tell you. Do we ever fucking sneak around. His house has become what I like to call our fortress.

"You just don't like that you're wrong," he tells me.

"Wow," I say, walking out to the nurses' station where everyone is talking. "Last patient of the day." I put the chart down on the pile. "I'm planning on soaking in a tub and going to bed at seven," I say, knowing we made plans to eat dinner tonight and watch a movie, which would usually end with us all over each other. In the past three weeks, nothing has changed. I want him just as much as I did that first day. Every single time, it gets better and better.

I walk out to my car, seeing that he is calling me. "Are you not making me dinner tonight?" he whispers. "You lost the bet."

"Rain check," I tell him as I get in the car.

"Really?" he says. "You're lying."

"I am not," I huff out even though I know I'm totally fucking lying. But I'm pissed that he won't even look at the facts.

"Liar, liar, pants on fire." He laughs, and it aggravates me.

"Fuck off," I tell him. "I'll speak to you tomorrow." I hang up, tossing my phone to the side while I drive home. I really do soak in the tub for what feels like an eternity. I have to say it isn't as nice as Gabe's tub, though. I get out, drying myself off, and see that he's called me four times. I'm about to call him back when the phone rings with Blake's name.

"Hey there," I say to him with a smile on my face. "How's my favorite cousin?"

"Tired as fuck." He laughs. "What are you up to?"

"Just got out of the bath and I'm heading to bed."

"It's fucking seven p.m." I look at the clock, smiling. "Don't tell me the country has got the city girl chilling out."

"You can say that." I laugh.

"So how is everything?" he asks. "How is Hailey doing?"

"Everything is fine," I tell him. "She's good. I think the best thing she ever did was move out here. Wait till you see her. It's not even like she's the old Hailey; she's the better Hailey."

"Really?" he says. "Good. I'm coming down tomorrow. I get off shift, and I'll drive right down, sleep during the day, and then make you take me out and show me the sights."

"You mean show you the street? It's basically one street." I laugh at him. "One street but with everything on it."

"Whatever." He laughs. "I'll see you when you get home from work."

"I can't wait," I say. Hanging up the phone, I go to find Hailey to tell her, but she isn't home. I go back upstairs, seeing that Gabe has called me three more times. I shake my head. "Nope," I say. "Not tonight."

My eyes flicker open when I hear something hit my window. I look that way, thinking maybe I dreamed it, but there it is again. I get up, looking out my window, and see Gabe tossing a pebble. I open my window. "What in the ever-loving fuck are you doing?" I ask as he stands there with his hands on his hips.

"Open the door." He walks toward the front door as I

close the window and walk downstairs to open the door.

"Are you out of your mind?" I ask him when he walks in, and I close the door. I don't have a chance to ask him again because he comes at me. His cold hands cup my face as he leans in and kisses me. My hands go to his hands on my face as I open my mouth for him. I move my hands to his head as he tilts his head to deepen our kiss. No matter how many times I've kissed him, it's always like the first time. His hands leave my face, traveling down my sides. He picks me up, and my legs wrap around his waist, our lips never separating as we continue to kiss. He walks me back upstairs to my room, falling on the bed with me. My hands frantic to get his t-shirt off. His hands now moving under my tank top where he cups my breast and plays with my nipple. I raise my hips to rub against him. My hand goes into the front of his pants, and I cup his cock, finding him already ready.

"Fuck," he hisses when I fist him and move up and down. He lifts my shirt, taking a nipple into his mouth, then sneaks his hand into the front of my shorts, his finger sliding between my folds as he mimics my hand movements.

"Gabe," I say breathlessly. "I need you." I release him, unsnapping his button and pushing his pants down over his hips.

"Condom?" he says, looking at me, his fingers still going in and out of me.

"Where is it?" I ask him.

"I don't have any," he says, and my eyes snap to his.

"What about in your wallet?" I ask him.

"Used it last week in the truck when you couldn't wait to get in the house," he says, his fingers still moving in me.

"Get off," I tell him, reaching around him to get into my nightstand drawer.

"You have one in there?" he asks me, now pulling down my shorts.

"No, but I have my vibrator," I tell him as his gaze snaps up and he watches me pull it out. "You got me all riled up, and I need relief."

He takes the vibrator from my hand and tosses it over his shoulder. "Over my dead body."

"If you don't fucking go pick up my vibrator, you will be dead."

"Are you on the pill?" he asks me. "I'm clean, very clean," he starts saying as he fists his cock in his hand.

"I'm on the pill," I lie to him, and it's sour in my mouth. "I'm clean. I've never done it without, and I got tested right before I moved here."

"So?" he asks me.

"Only this one time," I tell him and don't say anything else because he's already inside me.

"Fuck," he hisses. "Don't move or you really will need to get yourself off."

I wrap my legs around his waist, pushing his pants off with my feet, or at least lower than his hips. He pounds into me as his head comes down and kisses me. My fingers go through his short hair to his neck, pulling him closer to me. He gets on his elbows while our hips move toward each other. The whole time we never stop kissing, even when he buries himself inside me, and we both moan. We continue kissing until he slips out of me. He gets up, opening the bedroom door, and peeks out before going to the bathroom and coming back with a cloth for me to clean myself.

He kicks off his shoes and undresses, getting into bed with me. "How did you get here?" I ask him when he spoons me from behind.

"Cab." He kisses my neck. "Took fucking forever." I laugh but soon fall back asleep. When the alarm rings the next day, I expect to find him gone, but he's not. He's still beside me.

"Wake up." I nudge him. "Time to go."

He groans under protest, rolling over to continue sleeping. I get up to take a shower, and when I make it back to my bedroom, he's gone.

I walk downstairs, listening to him have a conversation with Hailey. "Fuck," I mouth.

"Your cousin wasn't answering her phone last night, so …" He starts talking, then I walk in.

"So he decided coming here at one a.m. and throwing rocks at my window was a good idea." I open the fridge, getting the milk out for the coffee and my lunch bag.

"I wouldn't have to do that if you had just answered your phone." He pours himself coffee.

"There was no need to answer my phone." I shrug, taking out some cereal and pouring it into a bowl.

"Because you hate being wrong." He points at me, and I glare at him, smashing the box of cereal on the counter.

"I'm leaving," I say, grabbing my purse, keys, and lunch bag. Turning to Hailey, I tell her, "Blake should be here late today. He called last night."

Hailey's face beams with a smile. "Oh, you answered his phone call!" Gabe says when he grabs his jacket and heads to the front door where I stand.

"Well, he isn't an asshole," I say, opening the front door. "How are you getting to work?" I ask him, and he throws his head back and laughs.

"You are going to drive me. I took a cab last night."

"I'm not showing up with you in my car." I turn to him. "People will see."

"And that's a problem because?" He puts his hands on his hips. "What's the matter, babe? Scared they might think you have a thing for me?"

I shake my head, laughing. "Trust me, the last thing I have is a thing for you."

"I'll remember that the next time you are beg—" I run to him, covering his mouth with my hand.

"Get in. I'm dropping you off at the corner. I'll slow down so you can tuck and roll." I turn around and walk away, not expecting him to smack my ass. I turn to glare at him now. "I won't even slow down now."

Gabe throws his head back, laughing as he gets in the car and leans over to kiss me. "You wouldn't hurt me," he says, and I just huff out when he takes my hand and brings it to his lips. Kissing my hand, he smiles at me. "Would you?"

"I guess we will see, won't we?" I say, pulling up to the clinic and looking around. Fuck, we arrived at the same time as Ava and Corrine. "Great," I hiss.

"Hey, guys, good morning," Gabe says as if us showing up for work together is a normal thing.

"Dr. Walker," Ava says shocked. "Crystal."

"His truck is in the shop, so I picked him up when he was walking," I tell them, walking in front of them.

"Thanks for the lift, but you have to drive me to pick up my truck at lunch. Please don't forget." I nod at him, smiling all the while I'm skinning his balls in my head. We walk in and go straight to work, only stopping at lunch when he asks me to drive him to pick up his truck. I smile at him while everyone else looks at us.

"You can't do that," I yell at him when we pull away from the clinic. "You could have asked anyone for a lift. Why me?"

"Well, besides the fact I like you and want to spend time with you?" he says, smiling at me. "I was hoping to get lucky." I turn, watching him while he wiggles his eyebrows.

"Not a chance in hell," I tell him. "You think I'm going to go back to the clinic with sex on my face? No."

"You really do glow after." He leans over, kissing my neck. I pull up while he unbuckles his seat belt. "You really aren't going to come in?"

"No, Gabe," I tell him. "I'm really not coming in."

I watch him walk up the steps to his house, and my heart is telling me to go in, live a little, but my gut tells me to turn around. I follow my gut; I always, always follow my gut.

I pull up to the clinic and am walking inside when my

phone rings, and it's Blake.

"Hey, did you get in?" I ask him.

"Something happened," he says, and my feet stop in the middle of the room. "Fuck," he says out loud. "I upset her. Do you know that guy she's dating?"

"Walker?" I ask. "Yes, why?"

"Call him and tell him to come to her; she needs him. She's sitting on the beach." I hang up on Blake right then, calling Walker right away.

"Where are you?" I ask him.

"Just got to the office," he tells me, and then asks, "what's the matter?"

"I have no idea, but Blake just called me and asked me to call you. I don't have the details," I say while I hear him peel out of the parking lot. Looking out the window, I see him take off. "But she's on the beach."

I look down at my phone when Gabe comes back in. "What's the matter?" he says, taking in my face.

"Not sure. Blake called and said Hailey is on the beach, so I called Walker."

"Whatever is the matter, Walker will fix it," he says, walking past me to the back, waiting for me to walk in front of him when he opens the door.

"I'm sure you're right," I say, tucking the phone into my pocket. He doesn't call me back, so I call him nonstop till he finally answers. "What the fuck is wrong with you two? Why can't you two carry phones?"

"Because they don't want you disturbing them." Gabe puts in his comments, but I turn around and hiss at him.

"Mrs. Henderson is waiting for you to treat her hangnail. I'm assuming you can do that without a nurse," I say to him, then go back to Walker. "What happened to Hailey?"

"I think it's best for her to tell you. I'm going to get Mila, and then we are meeting for dinner at D'Amore," he tells me, and I suddenly remember I didn't eat lunch.

"Oh, I want pizza. I'm coming too. At what time?" I ask him.

"I have no idea. Probably six," he answers.

"Perfect. I get off at that time, so save me a place."

"Me too," Gabe yells from the back. I spin around on my stool.

"You aren't invited," I tell him, glaring at him.

He stands there crossing his arms over his chest. "My cousin is going, so I can go to the restaurant if I want, Crys. It's a public place."

"Whatever, but you aren't sitting with us. Maybe you might meet another date?" I tell him, knowing full well it's a low blow.

"Oh my god, I dated her in fucking high school," he counters.

"I'm not talking to him. I'll be there. See you at six." I hang up. "So now you dated? You told me you were just friends."

He looks down at his feet and then up again. "It was one date."

"You're an asshole," I say under my breath, walking away from him. This man pushes my buttons more than anyone on this planet, and I have to make it stop. My

184

head is telling me it's time to cut the strings while my gut is telling me it's not.

Chapter Twenty-Four

Gabe

Fuck, the minute I said that I dated Felicia, I saw Crystal's face go from worried about her cousin to about to stab me in the eyeball with the pen in her hand.

I tried to get her to talk to me, but each time, she walked out of the room to a bunch of people. When the clock strikes six o'clock, I walk out of the office just as she is walking out. "Do you want to take one car there?" I ask her, and she answers with just one word.

"Nope." I know, I fucking know, this isn't going to bode well for any of us. Or at least me.

"I know you're probably pissed that I lied to you, but …"

"Oh, I'm not pissed you lied to me." She turns to look at me. "I mean, if I went out with Alan on a date once, and then by chance you saw me holding his hand the day after. And you asked me about it, and I told you we were just friends, but then you find out that I played tonsil hockey with him, it would be okay, right?"

"Did you fucking go on a date with Alan?" I ask her, my eyes now glaring at her. I'll fucking kill him. I'll break his fucking hands.

She throws her hands up. "You're incredible," she says, walking away to her car when she stops at mine. "Oh my god," she says, pointing at my tires.

"What the fuck is going on?" I say, getting down to see that they have been sliced again. I look around the parking lot. "This is insane. Someone is doing this on purpose."

"Well, you pissed off the wrong person, I guess," she says, getting into her car. "I can see how that could happen." As she closes the door, I open the passenger door, getting in the car and taking out my phone. "Get out."

"Just drive," I tell her. "Hey, Harrold," I tell my mechanic who answers the phone. "Can you send a tow to my office for my truck?"

"Sure thing. What's wrong with it?" he asks me.

"Someone sliced my tires again."

"Shit, you done pissed off the wrong woman this time." I close my eyes as I feel a headache beginning to form. "I'll call you in the morning."

We arrive at D'Amore right as I hang up the phone. "I'm putting a camera in my truck," I say to Crystal who walks in front of me.

"I'm not driving you home. I hope you know," she says as she looks around the restaurant for Hailey.

"You have to drive me home," I say while I follow her.

"Hey, there," Crystal says, sitting down next to Mila and kissing her cheek. "Hello, Princess. Blake."

"What happened to you?" Walker asks me when I sit in the chair next to him.

"Someone sliced my brand-new tires again," I say while I raise my hand to flag down the waitress. "Can I have two beers please?" I ask her and then look around at the table "Anyone else want anything?" Shrugging, I smile at her. "That's it."

"You ordered two beers?" Walker asks, laughing at me.

I put up both my hands. "I have two hands, and after the day I've had, I should have doubled that order."

Crystal picks up a menu and mumbles, "Maybe if you weren't such an a-hole, people wouldn't slice your tires." I don't bother to answer her. Instead, I just glare at her, but she turns and ignores me. That ass is going to be beet red tonight. I don't bother interacting with anyone or listening to Mila ask Blake questions about his job.

I've closed my eyes, pinching the bridge of my nose, when Hailey says she needs to go to the bathroom and so does Walker. The waitress places the beers in front of me.

"Well, isn't that convenient?" I say as I down one beer.

Walker pushes my shoulder when he walks by.

"Sorry, I didn't introduce myself." I lean over, extending my hand. "I'm Gabe. Walker's cousin and Crystal's—"

"Boss," Crystal finishes. "He's my boss."

"Nice to meet you." Blake shakes my hand, smiling. When the waitress comes back, we order a shit ton of food.

"Gabe has lived here his whole life," Crystal starts. "Dated a lot also." She looks at me. "Isn't that right?"

The meal runs smoothly till the bill comes and everyone fights for it. Well, everyone but me. I sit here glaring at Crystal while she smiles at me. I make a list in my head of how I'm going to torture her.

"Too late," I say. "I already paid the bill." I get up, looking at Crystal. "Let's go."

This doesn't bode well with her as she folds her arms over her chest. "I'm not driving you home."

I shake my head and think how pissed she would be if I just threw her over my shoulder. "Let's go." Then I hiss out, "Please."

"Fine." She throws her napkin on the table. "This is the last time." She grabs her purse, saying bye to everyone as we walk out.

"I was giving you till the count of ten and then I was fucking yanking you up and we were leaving," I tell her when I get in the car.

"Is that so?" she asks with a side look as she pulls into my driveway. "Get out," she says.

I lean over and turn the car off, taking the keys out of the ignition. "Not so fast. We need to talk."

I get out of the car, and she yells in frustration as she stomps up the steps. I walk straight to the kitchen and grab a bottle of water.

"Give me my keys." She stands there with her hand

outstretched. "Now."

"It was half a date," I say, crossing my ankles and leaning back against the counter. "Three hours, and it was a double date."

"I don't care," she says, not looking at me. "I want to go home."

"You care," I tell her, walking to her as she backs up until her back is pushed to the counter. "It's pissing you off how much you care." I push her hair from her face. "Because the thought of you with Alan or anyone else has my blood boiling."

I lean down to kiss her neck, where I know her heart beats. "I'd break his fucking kneecaps." I kiss the other side of her neck.

Her hands go from my chest to my neck. "Can you explain to me why one minute I want to run you over frontward and backward, and then the next, I want to kiss you till I have no more air left?"

"If I could explain that, you wouldn't have any use for me." I kiss her smile. "Now, I believe I owe your ass some attention."

"Is that so?" She arches to me.

"Fucking right." I pick her up, tossing her over my shoulder, and my palm connects with her ass, making even my palm sting.

I wake up the next morning to her alarm blaring, but she's nowhere to be found. I get up, calling her name. "Crys," I yell and then hear the shower turn on. I turn off her alarm and walk into the bathroom.

The shower doors are steamed from the heat of the

water. I open the door, stepping in with her, and she looks over her shoulder. "Don't," she tells me, but I'm too far gone. I smile, grabbing the bar of soap. Rubbing it between my hands, I then rub my hands on her breasts, lathering them with soap. Caressing them round and round as the water cascades over them. My cock aches for me to bend my knees and enter her. I kiss her neck when she grabs the soap from me and then reaches around to lather my dick.

"Fuck," I hiss, and by the time we get out of the shower, we have two minutes to leave the house. When we pull up together, I thank god no one is outside to see us, so we don't have to explain anything. The appointments are nonstop till I look up and see that it's seven thirty. I walk out and see that everyone has gone home. I take out my phone to call Crystal.

"Hello?" she says.

"Where are you?"

"I'm home getting dressed, why?"

"Because I'm going home, and I'm exhausted, and I don't feel like going out."

"Okay, so I'll see you tomorrow," she tells me.

"You are going to go out without me?" I ask her, shocked but not really.

"Well, I made plans, so I guess that would be a yes."

"Fine, whatever." I hang up the phone. "Why the fuck can't I find a woman who doesn't fucking piss me off half the time?"

I ask my truck as if the truck is going to answer.

I pull up to my house and walk inside, going straight

for the shower. I get out, shaving and putting on my boxers, then head downstairs to grab something to eat. Grabbing some leftover pizza, I sit at the island eating it while I scroll Facebook. I haven't been on in forever, and I see that Ava posted pictures of our retreat. Some are funny, the ones of me scowling especially, because fuck, did I hate that weekend. I find a good one of me and Crystal. Seeing that she is tagged in it, I go to her Facebook page. Her profile picture is of her looking at the camera and laughing, and she looks so, so happy. She also looks so beautiful. She is, without a doubt, hands down the most beautiful person I've ever seen inside and out. I save the picture to my camera roll and see a text come in from Brody.

I open it up and see it's a picture, my mouth opening at the picture he sent me. It's the back of Crystal, that is for sure. I would know that ass anywhere, but her fucking bare back is more than I can take. Another picture comes in, this time of the front with her laughing while she holds up a shot. I drop my phone when I see her fucking outfit.

She's standing in the tightest pair of fucking jeans ever made to mankind; it's almost like they are painted on. I mean tight,

which isn't the problem. It's the sheer black shirt she has on that is. It's obvious she isn't wearing a bra as it ties around her neck. Her breasts are covered by what looks like decals all sheer in the middle, tying around her neck. All ending with black strappy heels that make her legs look so much longer.

Another picture comes in, this time of Darla, Crystal, and Hailey dancing in the middle of the fucking bar. I roll my lips together, running upstairs two steps at a time. "I'm going to cut that top right down the middle," I say as I wrestle into a pair of dark jeans, grabbing a white button-down shirt and buttoning it while I grab a jacket, slide on my boots, and run to my truck. I think I make it there in record time. I open the door to the bar and see Brody's big smile when he spots me. "Asshole," I mutter. I walk toward them and try to keep my anger in check, but with this one, who the fuck can.

"What the fuck are you wearing?" I hiss, standing next to Walker while Brody laughs. Crystal turns around, putting a hand on her hip.

"An outfit." She glares at me.

"Is that right?" I ask, putting my hands in my back pockets, my eyes boring into her. My eyes roam up and down her, taking her in; my cock really fucking glad she is here.

"I think I need another shot," she says when she takes in my look.

"I'm so happy I didn't miss tonight," Darla says as they take another shot.

"I'm going to go to the bathroom," Hailey says, grabbing Crystal, and Darla follows them. Brody puts a beer bottle in my hand while my eyes never leave Crystal's back. Totally fucking see-through. Scissors are the only thing that comes to mind. That, or fucking ripping it in half. Either way, that shirt won't fucking survive.

I look around to see some people nod at me as I smile

and take a pull of the beer. Walker's receptionist comes over, and I swear I see heart emojis in her eyes directed right at him. I laugh because he hasn't been with anyone since his wife took off on him, and he's finally let Hailey in. It's safe to say he isn't letting that one go.

I watch the exchange between them. When Hailey returns, I see her realization that he's off limits. I don't care; my eyes go to Crystal who makes sure not to get too close to me.

"You want to dance?" I hear Walker ask Hailey, and I put my beer down and walk around them to Crystal.

"I thought you said you didn't want to come out to-night?"

she asks me as she looks around.

"You done?" I ask her as she looks up at me.

"I just got here," she says, smiling, then looking back at me. "But it's safe to say, I'm ready to leave." She winks at me. "I mean, that's if you can give a girl a lift." I shake my head, laughing at her. See, one minute I want to throttle her, and the next, I want to kiss her face till she melts in my arms. Crystal walks past me swinging her hips, and I make sure to follow right behind her so no one sees. I make it outside and look over my shoulder to see Walker watching me. I salute him while I point at where my truck is parked.

She gets in, buckling in, then turns her back to the door to look at me. "You're hot when you're all mad and irritated."

"Is that why you make me mad?" I ask her, pulling off and making my way to my house.

"No, I make you mad because it's easy to do." She laughs, leaning over to kiss my neck. I get out of the truck once I pull up to my house. Walking over to her side, I catch her right as she closes the door. I push her back against the truck door. Gripping her hips, I lean down and kiss her lips, tasting the tequila. She lunges forward to bite my lower lip, and I open my mouth, crushing down on hers. I pick her up, her legs wrapping around my waist, my cock perfectly aligned with her pussy as she rubs herself up and down on it. Her hands in my hair, around my neck, I feel her everywhere. I walk to the kitchen. She lets me go to moan, my mouth kissing her neck as I suck my way from right to left. I put her on the white marble island in the middle of the kitchen. Turning around, I open the drawer and grab exactly what I'm looking for.

"I was sitting here tonight"—I point at the stool I sat on—"going through Facebook." Her legs dangle while she leans back on one arm. "Found a picture of the two of us, and I sat there and thought fuck, is she beautiful, more than anyone I've ever met in my whole life." She looks at me smiling, my hand going on her leg as I trace my fingers up and down her thigh. "But then I got the fucking picture of your ass." I shake my head while she sits up, taking her forefinger to rub my cheek. "I knew it was your ass even before I knew it was you," I say. Grabbing one leg, I straighten it and then place the scissors under the hem, dragging them all the way up her thigh. I push her back down on the island and cut right through her waist. She looks at me with her mouth hanging open as I do the same to the other leg.

"You have lost your mind," she tells me when I pull her pants off her, and she sits on my island in nothing but that bodysuit. She points at me. "If you touch this top, I swear, you will not get any blow jobs for a month."

I laugh at her. She enjoys sucking my cock as much as I do. "Where did you get it from?" I ask her, leaning in to kiss her. With her lips on mine, I push her down on the island and then stand. She groans, and I look down at her, her eyes half glazed over. I run my finger down the middle of her top, my finger going over the mesh. "I like this top," I tell her while I unsnap it between her legs, leaving her pink pussy open and wet for me. I lean down, sucking on her clit. Her moans fill the room, then I stand back up and cut it right up the middle. "Now, I love it even more."

"You owe me two hundred dollars." She sits up as her top gapes open, her tits out for me to see. "And that is only for the top." She shakes her head when she grabs the shredded top.

"I'll give you fucking double," I tell her, tossing the scissors back into the drawer.

"You know this means no blow jobs for a month, right?" She crosses her arms, squeezing her tits together.

"Really?" I say, leaning down and taking a nipple into my mouth.

"I'm serious, Gabe." She starts out strong and then whispers, "One month."

"Okay," I tell her, grabbing her and bringing her to my room where I set her on my face, and she falls forward.

Her mouth lands right on top of my cock, and she takes me down her throat. I smile against her pussy. "That was the fastest month of my life."

She doesn't answer; she just takes me deeper into her mouth over and over again.

Chapter Twenty-Five

Crystal

"I can't move," I say, lying on the bed on my stomach. We have just finished our longest marathon sex session. Holy shit, I keep waiting for the day when I don't crave him or it isn't as good, but it's been over three months now, and I still get butterflies when he grabs my hand. My stomach still speeds up when he kisses me.

"Then don't move," he says, getting up to set the alarm.

"I'm not leaving. You don't have to keep setting it." I laugh, thinking back to the day I tried to sneak out, and the alarm that blared so loud he came running out naked.

"It's not for you," he says. "I'm tired of fucking buying new tires, and I've replaced the back window five times now."

I roll over. "Well, ever since you put the cameras up, it's been quiet, so maybe the scorned woman found another victim."

"There is no scorned woman; I dated maybe five girls my whole life," he says, coming back to bed. "My last girlfriend fled town at the thought of spending her life with me. I'm the scorned one."

My stomach falls when he says that as I think of him making vows to someone else. "Well, if she hadn't, you wouldn't have gotten the 'best blow job of your life.'"

He grabs my waist, bringing me closer to him and kissing my lips. "This is true; this is very true."

"See, so maybe her leaving wasn't so bad," I say, resting my head on his shoulder. "Would you do it again?"

"Yes," he says as he plays with my hand in his hand. "I want a wife and maybe a couple of kids."

My heart stops, my throat goes dry, and my hand on his stomach gets cold all of a sudden. "What about you?"

I breathe out. "Nope." I get up on my elbow. "No to both."

"Really?" he says, and his hand playing with my hair stops. "Why?"

"I've never wanted kids," I say nonchalantly as the words burn my mouth. "So getting married isn't that much of a goal."

"You'll change your mind," he says. "You'll get the itch," he says, laughing.

"No itch," I say and then turn over on my side, looking at my bag on his chair in his bedroom, blinking away the lurking tears. "What time is the dinner tomorrow?" I ask him about the team dinner we are having.

"We have to be there at seven," he says, turning to hug me and kiss my shoulder. "You brought clothes, right?"

"Yup," I say, faking a yawn. "Goodnight."

"Night, doll face," he says, kissing my neck as I listen to him drift off to sleep. My eyes watch the stars blinking in the sky. *He's going to get married one day*, I think to myself. My stomach feels as if someone just kicked me. He's going to lie in this bed with another woman and make babies. I get out of bed, going to the bathroom. Closing the door, I allow the tears to fall. "Next week," I tell myself. "Next week, I'll let him go."

I walk back to the bed, getting back under the covers. Placing my head on his chest, I feel his arm coming around to hug me. "You okay?" he mumbles.

"Yeah, fine," I answer when he kisses my forehead. I close my eyes and listen to his heartbeat, falling into a rough night's sleep.

"Are you almost ready?" I hear Gabe yell from downstairs.

"Yes," I yell, pulling on my white jeans, the waist tighter than usual. "Fuck, I need to start working out," I say, grabbing the light peach shirt that matches. I slip it over my head, pulling it down on my shoulders. Thank god, the shirt flows around so I can leave the jeans unbuttoned. I slip on the brown heels and head downstairs. "My pants don't fit me," I say once I get into the living room. I lift my shirt to show him that I can't button my jeans.

"Where is the rest of your shirt?" he asks while I look at him. He's wearing tight blue slacks with a white button-down shirt with blue lines and a gray thin sweater on top, which molds to his chest. His sleeves pushed up.

"What's wrong with my shirt?" I say, looking down.

"Your shoulders are all out," he says, leaning down and kissing one. "You should become a nun, so I won't have to glare at anyone when they look at you."

I throw my head back and laugh. "Let's go before you cut this shirt, too." I walk to the door with him grabbing my ass. "You need to stop that. We are going out in public."

He groans. "I fucking hate this shit. We really need to negotiate that rule."

I walk down the stairs still laughing. "It's the only rule we have."

He opens his door and gets in. "No, we also have the no sleepovers on a work night."

I lean over to kiss him. "Okay, fine. We can throw out the sleepover rule."

"Really?" he asks all happy.

"No, but we could think about it," I say while he grabs my hand. "Are we picking up anyone else?"

"Nope," he says, turning down the street and reaching to turn on the radio. I look out the window at the water crashing into the shore.

When we get to the restaurant, I make sure not to walk too close to him, especially once we make it to the table where Ava and Corrine are waiting for us. "Hey," I say while they both look at us. "You guys the only ones here?"

"Yes, Emma just texted that she and Mia are carpooling together, and Alan is going to be picking up Olivia."

"Perfect," I say, sitting down in the chair facing them.

Gabe pulls out the chair next to me and sits down.

"This place is supposed to be good," he says, grabbing the menu. "Brody brought Darla here for their anniversary."

"Aww, isn't that sweet," Ava says. "They are so cute. That is relationship goals."

"Word," Corrine says. "How long have they been married?" she asks Gabe who puts his menu down.

"I think five years," he says, grabbing the glass of water and drinking from it.

"I swear, their kids are going to be the cutest in the world," Ava says. "I can't wait to have kids."

"Really?" Gabe asks.

"Oh, yeah, I've wanted to be a mother since I was a little girl. I used to wrap bags of carrots in a blanket and pretend it was a baby."

We all laugh. "I mean, I want kids," Corrine says, "but like not now *now*. Maybe in about five years, ten max."

I nod at them. "I guess I'm the opposite," I tell them. "I never want kids."

"Really?" Ava says, and then Emma and Mia arrive.

"Hey. Sorry we are late," Mia says, sitting in front of us next to Corrine and Ava. "What were you guys talking about?"

"Kids," Gabe says, putting his hand on my chair and stretching out his arm. "Crystal doesn't want kids."

I wait for the onslaught of opinions. "Well, it's not for everyone," Emma says. "I didn't want them either, but then well, one slipped by." She smiles.

"I would die," I say, grabbing my water and drinking

it. Thankfully, Alan and Olivia arrive with Gabe's parents right behind them. The rest of the meal goes smoothly, and Gabe stays quiet most of the night, not really part of any conversation. When we get into the truck later that night, he looks over at me.

"What's wrong with you?" I look over at him.

"Nothing, just thinking," he says. "You coming over or going home?" he asks, and I know he's pissed about something because he never gives me the option.

"Home please," I say, not bothering with the conversation. My heart beats fast in my chest as we get closer and closer to my house. I slam the truck door as soon as we pull up to the house, going up the steps with my head down.

"You really mean it, don't you?" Gabe yells from beside the truck. "You really don't want children?"

I inhale a big breath and gear my heart up for battle.

Turning around, I take him in, his shirt rolled up at the wrists, his dark slacks perfect. What I would give for just one more kiss. But I knew this day would come, knew in my heart I would have to say goodbye to him one day. I just didn't think today would be the day. I walk down one step. "I really, really don't want children."

He puts his hands in his pockets. "There must be a reason," he says, looking up at the sky. "There must be."

"There is nothing," I say, my voice raising just a little, but enough for him to stop. "I don't want kids; I've never wanted kids." Lies, all fucking lies. From when I was five years old and my mother bought my first baby, I've wanted to be a mother.

"But," he says, looking at me, "I do." Two words shatter me, two words I wish I could give him.

"Then go have them." I raise my hand to him. "No one is stopping you."

"You!" he yells out so loud I hear the front door open behind me, and Hailey steps out.

"Is everything okay?" she asks as I say yes and Gabe says no.

"You are the one stopping me because I love you," he says, not moving from his side of the truck. "I'm in love with your cousin, so in love with her that I can't put it into words, but …"

I take a deep breath. "I'm sorry," I say, and his head snaps back. "I'm sorry that you feel that way. I'm sorry that it has come to this."

"You're sorry?" he roars. "You're fucking sorry. For what?"

"Gabe," Hailey says, coming to stand next to me, holding my hand. "Maybe now isn't the right time."

"It's time," I whisper to her. "It went on too long."

"It went on too long? What the fuck are you talking about? Did we have an expiration date that I didn't know about? For fuck's sake, I just told you I love you, and all you can say is you're sorry. You're fucking sorry." He shakes his head. "I want to have kids with you; I want to have a future with you; I want it all with you."

"You can't have it," I tell him as a tear rolls out the corner of my eye.

"Because you won't let me. You won't let us," he yells at the top of his lungs.

"I'm infertile," I say the two other words that shattered me when I was nineteen. I say them out loud to the two people I love more than I love myself. The two people I would give my life for. My cousin squeezes my hand and gasps while Gabe just looks at me, shock in his eyes. "I was told at nineteen that I was infertile. I would never have children. My body was nineteen, but my insides were not." I let the tears fall, finally unleashing it. "So no, I can't give you what you dream; I can't even give myself what I dream because it's impossible. So you can stand there and tell me that you love me, you can stand there now and tell me it's going to be okay, but it's not. It will never be okay." I let go of Hailey's hand and turn to go up the step, looking back at the man I love. I would do anything to make his dreams come true, but I'm not that woman. "So that is why I'm sorry. I'm sorry I can't give you what you want. I'm sorry that no matter how many times I cried those tears, nothing in my body has changed. I'm sorry that no matter how much I prayed, no matter how much I begged God to just give me a chance, to just let me prove how good of a mother I can be, he didn't listen," I say, watching him and taking in his face. I turn around. "Goodbye, Gabe," I say, walking into the house and going to the couch, my body numb.

Hailey comes right in after me, the sound of his truck leaving blocked off when she closes the door. I don't turn to look at her; I keep my eyes focused ahead, keep looking at that little brown speck on the coffee table. She sits next to me, her arms going around my shoulders. "I love him," I say, finally turning to her as tears run down both our faces. "I love him so much my heart hurts," I whisper, laying my head on her shoulder. "Why?" I don't know what I'm asking. "Why?" I finally let the sob roar through me. "Why?" I cry into her arms as she rocks me, our tears mixing.

"I don't know why," she finally says as my sobs continue. We stay on the couch, and I cry out with the pain of losing myself all over again. I did the one thing I told myself not to do—I fell in love. She holds me all night long till morning. She takes my phone and calls into work, telling them I'm sick.

Chapter Twenty-Six

Gabe

When she walked into her house, slamming the door, I walked to the steps, but Hailey stopped me. "She won't listen to what you have to say. Not now."

"I'm not leaving her now," I told her, but she just nodded her head.

"She is the strongest person I know. When my husband died, she would have carried me and my pain on her shoulders, and she did," she said. "She actually confronted Eric's wife."

"She can't believe I'd just leave her." The thought that she would go to bed thinking I would just leave her is too much. My heart breaks for her; the fact she kept this a secret and bore it alone ... I can't even think what that must have felt like.

"If you go in there, she will only push you away faster than she did before. Give her a couple of days."

"I'm giving her two, but that's it. Then I'm coming

back. I don't give a flying fuck what anyone says." I get in my truck and take off with tears in my eyes. I pull up at Walker's, knocking on the door, and then walk in.

I walk past him to his scotch, taking three big gulps, only stopping when the burning gets too much. "What the fuck is wrong?" he asks worried, not moving from his spot.

"She can't have kids," I whisper. "And I want to have babies with her." I turn around.

"What?" he says, his voice low.

"Even with Bethany, I knew it would come, but I just didn't think of it. But with Crystal, it's the only thing I think of. She's so soft, sweet, and kind," I say, taking another swig. "I told her I loved her, and then told her that I wanted kids, and she told me she's infertile."

"Oh my god." His hands go to his mouth.

"I don't give a shit anymore. I don't care if she can have kids or not. I just want her."

"You can't just make that decision," he tells me, and I shake my head.

"The thought of having a child with someone else makes my skin crawl. The thought of living without her hurts my chest. Like a physical pain," I say, drinking another shot.

"I can't breathe without her." I walk to the couch, pressure on my chest. "I can't do it."

"Why are you here?" he asks me. Sitting next to me, he grabs the bottle from me. "Why are you not with her?"

"Because besides all those good things about her, she is stubborn, so fucking stubborn, and I know she won't listen to anything I have to say today. Nothing."

"So you have a plan?" he asks me, and I shake my head.

"No fucking idea. All I know is that I'm giving her two days, two days to get her shit together, and then I'm going after her."

"You think she'll listen to you?"

"My father was right. I didn't love Bethany. I didn't go after her; I didn't even think to go after her. With Crystal, I know I won't let her live without me."

"We'll get her back," he says, and I sit here in the dark with him by my side. My eyes never close the whole night, my chest in so much pain that I keep rubbing it.

"Uncle Gabe, you had a sleepover?" Mila asks when she walks into the kitchen the next morning and sees me still sitting on the couch.

"Yes." I smile at her when Walker bends and picks her up, telling her good morning. He kisses her neck, and she squeals and looks at him as if he hung the moon and the stars. I want that; I want it more than I can explain, but I want her more. I want Crystal more than I want kids. I get up from the couch, my phone beeping in my pocket. I rush to get it out to see that she called in sick.

"I'm going home. I need to shower before work," I tell Walker who nods at me. "One more day," I say to him as he nods.

Going home is worse than it was ever before. She left her things over yesterday. Her t-shirt that she wore yesterday morning is strewn across the bed. I pick it up and bring it to my nose, smelling her. Turning to sit on the bed, I slump my shoulders, my head down.

Getting up is almost impossible, and the day ahead is more painful. I smile when I need to, but it's clear I'm not myself when even Olivia bails on me and sends in Mia.

I spend as much time at the office as I can, but even here, she's everywhere. My phone rings with a weird number. "Hello," I say.

"It's Hailey," she whispers. "Can you talk?"

"Yes," I answer her, knowing she's my lifeline to my woman.

"She's coming in tomorrow. But," she says, and I hear her inhale, "this is going against everything that we stand for. Usually, it's us against the world, but," she says and sniffles, so I know she's crying, "but she needs her happy. She deserves her fucking happy, and a man who loves her more than he loves himself."

"I do," I answer, cutting her off.

"I think she's going to leave."

My heart speeds up, my palms sweaty and the phone almost slips out of my hands. "Leave? Leave to where?"

"Home," she says. One word.

"This is her home," I counter.

"Well, that answers all my questions. Now you need to convince her of that," she says. "I have to go. She's coming." And she hangs up.

I text her instead of calling her back.

Text me if she leaves before tomorrow.

When I finally make it home, I don't bother going upstairs to the bed. I fall asleep on the couch, hoping that it goes fast, and I can see her sooner. When I walk into the office the next day, I hear the nurses talking about how sick she looks, so they placed her in the chart room. I walk toward the chart room but am stopped by Ava with an emergency, so I go into the exam room, rushing to get to Crystal, but the universe has other plans for me. Because every single time I take a step forward to her, it pushes me back. I hiss out every single time someone tells me I'm needed. I'm standing in the exam room when I hear my name shouted.

"Dr. Walker." I hear Emma shout. Walking out of the room, I finally see her, her eyes with dark circles around it, her face pale, so pale. Her lips even paler. She looks at me, but it's like she doesn't see me as she starts going down. I run to her, catching her right before she hits the floor.

Chapter Twenty-Seven
Crystal

I gave myself yesterday; I gave myself a day to mourn.
I don't look at my phone; I don't pick it up when work
calls to check on me; I don't pick it up when I think it's
Gabe. I don't look at it. I drift in and out of sleep all day,
never moving from the couch. My body feels broken, it
aches all over, but the worst pain is in my chest. My heart
hurts, and no amount of pressure I apply to my chest
makes it go away. The next day, I get up and continue my
day. I walk in, looking down when they ask if I'm feeling
better. "Getting there," I say, going to my locker. I get to
the nurses' station, and Mia takes one look at me. "You
still look like you're fighting something, so why don't
you work in the chart room today?"

"Thank you so much," I say, going into the room
where we keep all the charts. If the patient is coming in,
I pull their files. The morning goes by slow, and I hear
Gabe's voice a couple of times and hold my breath. I

pick up my phone and call my grandmother, who picks up after one ring.

"Well, well, well," she says, and I close the door.

"Hey, Nanny," I say quietly.

"What's the matter? What happened?" she says.

"I think I need to come home," I say, my lips quivering. "It's time to come home."

"I'll come down and get you," she says. "I'll be there tomorrow."

"Okay," I say quietly. I wipe a tear away. "I love you."

"Be strong," she says and then disconnects. I put my phone back in my pocket. Taking a deep breath, I walk out of the room, my stomach rumbling as I walk past the nurses' station.

"Why is it so hot in here?" I ask as the back of my neck gets hot. I put the pen down on the nurses' desk, turning around. The sound of my heartbeat echoing in my ears.

I need to drink some water, maybe some juice. "Are you okay?" Emma asks as I turn to walk to the staff room, but I turn back to look at her. My head turns slowly as I see spots of black around. "Dr. Walker." I hear being yelled. I hear commotion all around me when my legs give out, and I fall to the floor.

"What's wrong with her?" I hear Gabe yelling.

"She was complaining about the heat." I hear Emma say and feel my body being lifted and laid on a table.

"I want a cold cloth." I hear Gabe say, and my eyes open. My stomach feels like I'm going to be sick.

"I think I'm going to be sick," I say softly, blinking

open my eyes.

"You're awake," Gabe says, coming to my side and brushing my hair from my face.

"Step aside, son." I hear Dr. Walker Sr. say.

"I'm not going anywhere," he hisses.

"Calm down," he tells him, coming to me. "Okay, what happened?"

"She fainted," Gabe yells from next to me, his face now white as the worry sets in. He comes to my side, holding my hand and bringing it to his lips.

His father looks at him and smiles. "Well, this answers a whole bunch of questions." He smiles at me. "Now, Crystal, tell us what happened."

"I'm fine." I try to get up and my head pounds, so I lie back down. "I'm just hungry. I haven't eaten today or actually yesterday. I wasn't feeling well." I avoid making eye contact. "I'm sure once I eat something, I'll be fine."

Dr. Walker takes my blood pressure. "It's a little high, but considering all this commotion, that's normal. I'm going to order some blood work just to be safe," he says, calling Mia. "Is there anything else you feel besides the hot flash?" he asks, taking his stethoscope to listen to my heartbeat. "Breathe in through your nose, out through your mouth."

"That sounds good," he says and then moves to my stomach, palpating it, and I hiss in pain. "Have you had stomach tenderness before today?"

I shake my head, looking up at Gabe, his face still white. "Get the ultrasound machine," he yells.

"Son, you really need to calm down." He walks over

to him. "She's fine."

The door opens when Emma comes in with the ultra-sound machine. "She looks a bit better." She hands me some apple juice. "Thought you could use some sugar maybe."

"Thank you." I reach out and take it from her, finishing it all in one shot. "This is silly, Dr. Walker. I already feel better."

"Dear." He looks at me, then at his son. "For everyone's sake, why don't we just humor him?"

"Fine, but no blood test," I say, closing my eyes.

"We'll see," he says, folding his arms over his chest.

Dr. Walker turns off the lights and comes over to me on his stool. I raise my top and lower my scrub bottoms a bit. He squeezes the blue gel on my stomach, places the wand on my stomach, and we all look at the black screen.

I don't know what I'm looking for, but what I get isn't what I was expecting. "Oh, well." I hear him say as I look at the screen. The picture on the little monitor has me mesmerized because it's impossible. Tears flow down my cheeks, and I don't even care. "I'm not a professional, but I'd say that's a baby."

"It can't be," I whisper. "I'm infertile."

"I can assure you that isn't the case." He laughs, moving the machine around on my stomach, and we see two feet and two hands.

I look at Gabe, who has his own tears coming down his face. "A baby." He looks at the screen, and his father turns on the sound. The sound of horses galloping fills the room. And I laugh. Joy, complete and utter joy.

My heart feels like it's going to come out of my chest. "They told me that I would never have kids, that my body was going into menopause when I was nineteen." I look at Gabe. "They said I would never be able to have children. I have no eggs."

"Well, I can happily say they are wrong," Dr. Walker says.

"I can't believe this," I whisper, my eyes never leaving the screen.

"Just so you know, I wasn't going away. I was giving you today, then I was coming for you." He comes close to kiss my lips softly. "We're having a baby." And I lose it and sob while he holds me.

"I think I'll give you two a minute," his father says. Grabbing his son on his shoulder, he says, "Congratulations, son."

He grabs my hand, kissing it. "I don't think I've ever been so happy."

"Can you check again?" I ask him. "Just to make sure."

"Anything," he says, grabbing the machine and turning it on. The sound of the heartbeat fills the room again. "Let us see what we have here." The baby flips over from back to front, and I actually feel flutters. "I wonder how far along you are?"

"I have no idea. I haven't gotten my period in at least six years." Looking at the monitor, he presses a couple of buttons.

He closes down the machine and turns on the light.

"How are you feeling?" he asks, coming over with a towel to wipe off my stomach. He then leans down and kisses the baby. "I love you," he says, and I run my hand through his hair.

"I'm going to be a mother," I say, smiling so big my cheeks hurt as the emotions overcome me. "I'm going to have a baby." I sob, holding my mouth as joy fills me. "A mother. I'm going to be a mother."

"Yeah, baby." He kisses me. "The best mother. Now, let's get you home." I nod, getting up. "Are you dizzy? Do you want me to get a wheelchair?"

"No. Hell no, I just need your hand." I reach out for his hand, and we walk out, holding hands.

I look at the nurses' station, seeing that they called Hailey, who stands with tears in her eyes, mixed with fear while Walker holds her shoulders.

I smile at her when she starts to walk to us but stops when Gabe yells, "We're having a baby." He raises our hands as I shake my head while everyone looks shocked.

"Maybe we should have started with we're dating and then ease in." I smile but stop when Hailey gets to me.

Her hands go to my face as she wipes tears away. "You're having a baby?" she cries as I nod my head. "A baby." She takes me in her arms, and I sob again, holding her. "A miracle," she says between sobs, and Walker comes to her side.

The room has cleared out, and it's just the four of us. "I came as soon as I could." I hear Mrs. Dr. Walker walk into the back room, her husband coming out of his office. "Oh my god, Crystal, are you okay? They told me you fainted?" She walks to me. "Why is she crying?" She looks around at her husband who smiles big.

"We're having a baby," Gabe says next to me, pulling me to him. My arms go around his waist, and I look up at him smiling. "A baby."

She gasps, her hands going to her mouth. "I knew it." She turns to look at her husband. "I told you."

"What?" I ask shocked

"Oh, honey, it was so apparent, and not even all from you, but from him." She points at her son. "It was in his eyes. He would follow you when you weren't looking, would find you in a crowd of people." She smiles. "I'm going to be a grandmother." She puts her hands on her chest. "It's a girl. I feel it."

"Everyone needs to calm down and give her space," Gabe says. "We need to get her into bed, so she can rest."

"Yes," his mother says, agreeing. "Someone get a wheelchair."

"Oh my god," I whisper to myself, but the smile never leaves my face. Especially when I call Nanny that night and tell her the big news, oh and that I'm staying right where I am.

Chapter Twenty-Eight

Gabe

"Do you want me to carry you inside?" I ask her when we pull up to my house.

"No." She turns, looking at me with a smile, the same smile that hasn't left her face since she saw our baby. We walk into the house with our hands together, her stomach growling. "I'm hungry."

"Yes," I say, turning her to face me. "I missed you," I say, holding her face in my hands. "So much," I whisper when I lean down and kiss her gently.

We don't move from the door when the bell rings. Pulling open the door, we see Brody and Darla with food in their hands. "We came as soon as they called." I look at them with confused eyes.

"Oh my god," Darla says, coming inside, "I'm so, so happy for you guys." She hugs first me and then Crystal.

"No," I say loudly, "you can't stay. She needs to get off her feet and rest."

"Gabe," Crystal says, grabbing my arm and pulling me close, "they brought food, and I'm hungry." I look at her.

"Twenty minutes," I say while Darla and Brody walk to the kitchen, but then the door opens again. This time, it's Hailey, Walker, and Mila. "What is this? My woman needs to get off her feet and rest."

Hailey laughs. "She may be your 'woman,'" she says, making air quotes with her fingers, "but she was my cousin first." She walks to Crystal, hugging her as they both cry in each other's arms.

"This isn't keeping her calm," I tell them when Walker pushes me by the shoulder, walking to the kitchen. "Enough," I say to them as they tear apart. "Her blood pressure must be skyrocketing right now. It's not good."

"Oh, dear," Hailey says, leaving us to walk into the kitchen where I hear everyone laughing and celebrating.

"You need to calm down just a bit." Crystal comes to me. "They are just happy for us."

"It's …" I say, almost stomping my feet. "I haven't been with you in two days."

She leans up, kissing my jaw. "You'll have all the alone time with me later. Besides, we have to have make-up sex."

"We aren't having sex until the doctor clears you." I put my hands on my hips, and I swear I hear my cock moan.

"You are a doctor." She turns, walking away and looking at me over her shoulder. "So you can clear me."

As she sways her hips, I look up at the ceiling and

start counting to ten, so my cock could compose itself. When I walk into the kitchen, she is sitting on a stool, eating a big plate of lasagna that they brought. I stand here with Brody on one side and Walker on the other while I look over at Crystal as she eats, her eyes glowing with happiness.

When everyone finally leaves, which is about one hour later than my timeframe, I carry her upstairs, her head on my shoulder. "We need to call a doctor and make an appointment," she says, kissing my neck.

"Already done," I tell her. "He's actually coming to the practice tomorrow morning at nine."

"How?" She raises her head and looks at me. "When?"

"The minute I saw that baby on the screen, I told my father and he pulled some strings. Dr. Sprung is coming in for us."

"As in the fertility god doctor?"

"Yup," I say, placing her on the bed. "He and Dad go way back. He owes dad a favor, so he called it in."

She sits up, propping herself against the pillows. "He's impossible to get into."

I smile. "Well, tomorrow morning we have an appointment with him." I lean over and kiss her.

"I didn't lie to you," she whispers, her hand coming out to touch my lower lip with her thumb. "I would never trap you like that."

"Trap me?" My eyebrows squeeze together. "What the hell are you talking about?"

She looks down and then looks up again. "We'd just met, and I get it. People might think I did this on purpose. I really don't care." She moves her hand down to her stomach. "You didn't ask for this, so if you don't want it, I understand."

"What?" I whisper, placing my hand on her stomach. "When you walked away from me and slammed the door, I was coming after you, but Hailey, she told me what I didn't want to see. That you needed time, that we both needed time to get our thoughts together." She blinks, and tears fall over her lids. "I went to Walker's and sat on his couch the whole night, and the only conclusion I came to was I couldn't live without you." I smile at her, and my thumb catches one tear. "So I don't give a flying rat's ass what anyone says. We are having a baby." I put my hand on her stomach.

"Yeah, we are." She nods her head and smiles, her hand going to mine. "We are having a baby."

I spend the night listening to her breathing, my hand cradling her stomach.

We walk into the office the next day holding hands. "Good morning, everyone," I say to the nurses at the station when I walk to my office, and she goes to her locker. "Dr. Walker." I hear Mia say, "Dr. Sprung is waiting in your office."

"Thank you, Mia. Can you send Crystal in when she comes out?" I tell her, going to my office and opening the door. Dr. Sprung sits on the couch, looking at his phone typing away.

"Dr. Sprung," I say, going to him with my hand outstretched, "I'm Gabriel Walker."

He gets up, shaking my hand. "Gabe, nice to meet

you." The door opens, and Crystal comes in. "This must be the mother."

"Dr. Sprung, this is my fiancée, Crystal." Her head snaps to me. "Later," I whisper as she reaches out to shake his hand.

"Thank you so much for coming on such short notice," she tells him.

"Well, why don't we get started, shall we?" He points at the door, and we go into the exam room. "If you will undress from the waist down, we'll get started in just a bit," he says, going outside to give us some privacy.

"Fiancée?" she hisses. "Really?"

"Can we possibly do this tonight, and not before we see our baby?"

She points at me. "It's no, I won't marry you," she says, her scrubs falling to the floor as she grabs a white sheet and places it on her lap. The knock on the door stops her from almost yelling at me.

"Okay." He comes in with a paper in front of him. "Why don't we start at the beginning?"

"At nineteen, my period stopped. I went three months without, so I went to my OB/GYN. I thought the stress of nursing school and working full time had just knocked my system off a bit."

She looks down at her hands and then up again. I walk to her side, sitting next to her, and hold her hand. "Well, he did a couple of routine tests. He called me back in to tell me that I had no eggs. My body was nineteen, but my reproductive system wasn't." I bring her hand to my mouth. "Every year, I would go in for routine tests and always ask if anything had changed. They didn't."

"So your last menstrual cycle was when?" he asks while he writes notes on his paper.

"Six years ago, maybe seven," she says, and he goes to place his paper down. Grabbing gloves, he says, "Okay, lie back. I'm going to do an internal exam, and then we'll get an ultrasound to see what's going on."

She lies down, putting her feet in the stirrups that Dr. Sprung pulled up from the sides of the table. He examines her. "Everything is where it should be." He takes off his gloves, rolling to the light switch and flipping it off. "Let's see what we have," he says, squeezing the blue gel on her stomach, and he places the wand on her. The sound of the galloping fills the room again as both of us look at the screen. "Strong heartbeat," he says, moving around her stomach. "Active little one," he says. "I'm trying to get the length, and it's almost impossible." He laughs. "I see a stubborn little one. A very stubborn one." He clicks a couple of things. "Okay, so from what I can see, you're about fourteen weeks along. So you are over the twelve-week scary mark. Do you guys want to know what you're having?"

"You can tell?" she asks, looking at me. "Do we want to know?"

"It's up to you, doll face." I smile at her.

"I don't want to know because it doesn't matter as long as he or she is healthy." She looks at Dr. Sprung.

"So far, everything looks like it's in place, ten fingers and ten toes." He smiles. "But now comes the bad news of sorts."

My heart stops. "What?" Crystal whispers.

"Well, considering what you told me, I would have to say that this is technically a high-risk pregnancy. So"—he wipes off her stomach—"she should be off her feet for at least the next month, just in case, and I want to see her weekly to make sure everything is growing okay." He smiles. "Then we will go from there."

"So I'm having a baby?" she cries. "Like, it's not a dream?"

"Not a dream, Crystal. You're having a baby." He smiles. "I'll be in your office," he says to us as he walks out.

"Holy shit, I'm going to be a mother." She puts her hand over her face as she cries out tears of happiness.

Chapter Twenty-Nine

Crystal

Walking out of the room after Dr. Sprung left us, Gabe says, "You can't work today, so you should go home and rest."

"I can do paperwork," I tell him, approaching the nurses' station.

"Oh, good. Dr. Walker, Ava just called in sick," Mia says.

"See, I can do the board while Mia helps you."

"The doctor said …" I put my hand on his lips, shushing him.

"I swear, if at any time I feel tired or anything, I will stop. I can even do it on the computer, so I can sit down."

I look at him, and fuck is he ever hot. He hasn't shaved this morning, so his beard has grown out a touch, the white dress shirt is open at the neck, showing me a little of the ink he has there. His dark blue slacks hugging him. "You'd better stop that," he says, lifting his hand to fix his collar.

"You're hot," I tell him. "Have I ever mentioned how hot you are?" I smile and then walk to his office to finish my appointment.

Sitting in the chair next to Dr. Sprung, he goes over my dos and don'ts. "Okay, here is a list that I made. No exercise at all, not to lift anything over five pounds, no sex, no baths/hot tubs, etc. No swimming, no sleeping on your stomach. Also, no sushi."

"When you say no sex …" I ask him as he smiles. "What does that mean?"

"It means no penetration and no oral either. For her." He smiles at Gabe. "Basically, just lie around and take it easy."

"Can she work?" Gabe asks with his hands over his chest.

"Not on my feet, sitting at the desk."

"No," he says, shaking his head. "That's a no. I also want you taking a prenatal vitamin."

"Get ready. I'm going to drive you home," Gabe says to me while Dr. Sprung stands. "So we will come see you in one week."

He smiles at us. "I look forward to it."

"Thank you so much, Dr. Sprung." I smile while I shake his hand.

"I'll be back in an hour," Gabe says to everyone while we walk out. "Where do you want to go?"

"Well, home," I say, getting in the truck.

"Are you going to pack up your stuff and move in?" He looks at me as he drives out of the parking lot.

"Why would I move in with you?" I say. "I don't even like you most of the time."

"Well, half of me is inside you," he says with a huge grin on his face, "so technically, you have to like me."

I roll my eyes. "Drop me off at my house, and we will see if I see you before I have to." He pulls up to the house, and I open the truck door, stepping out when his phone starts ringing.

"Hello," he says while I walk ahead of him to the door. "What do you mean my house is on fire?" I turn around to watch him. "I'm on my way."

"My house is on fire," he says, jogging back to the truck. I get in as soon as he does. "What are you doing?"

"I'm coming with you. If I stay here, I will worry, and if I worry, it's stressful, which is not what I need."

"You find loopholes with everything, don't you?" He smiles at me.

"I have no idea what you mean." I shrug my shoulders as we make it to his house. Two firetrucks are working on it, and it looks almost as if it's his whole house. We get out of the truck in shock as the orange flames are coming out of the windows upstairs. "Oh my god," I say, walking toward the barricade.

"Hey," Gabe says to the cop blocking our entrance. "What is going on?"

"No clue, got a call from a neighbor," he says. "Fire department got here as soon as they could."

We watch in horror as his house burns; the fire department finally gets it under control, but it's safe to say that nothing survived. The fire chief comes to us while we sit in the truck, waiting.

"Dr. Walker." He comes over, taking off his helmet. "We have the fire under control. Luckily, no one was hurt, but we have to say we suspect arson."

My eyes become as big as saucers as I listen to him tell us about how the fire started. "Nothing could be saved."

"Do you think the person slashing your tires is also the one who set your house on fire?" I ask him when a detective approaches us.

"Dr. Walker," he says, coming to us, "I'm sorry to do this to you now, but we have someone in custody."

"Who?" Gabe says, pushing off the truck. "Who the fuck is doing this?"

"Ava Mitchell."

"What?" I say shocked. "It's impossible; she works with us."

The cop looks at Gabe and then down at the ground. "Oh my god, were you having sex with her?" I ask him, and he gasps.

"Are you insane?" he says. "I've never fucking touched her."

"Mr. Walker is correct, but it seems that Ms. Mitchell is in love with you." He points at Gabe. "According to her, you secretly love her, but then you got your mistress pregnant."

"She's lying," Gabe says. "She has worked for me for three years. I was engaged to someone else just seven months ago." He runs his hands through his hair. "I never, ever gave her any reason to think I wanted anything from her, ever."

"We are going to charge her, and I would like for you to come down to the station and make an official statement," he says, walking away.

"I'm beyond exhausted," I say, getting into the truck, "but we need to get this over with."

"You're not coming with me." He looks over at me. "There is no fucking way in hell I'm going to let her get anywhere near you."

"I'm not letting you go there by yourself," I tell him.

"Well, I'm dropping you off at home. Hailey is going to be there with you, and Walker is going to come with me."

"I want to come with you."

"And I want you safe," he says, pulling up to my house. "I want you and the baby safe, and being safe means nowhere near her."

"Fine," I agree finally, "but I don't want her near you either. She's obviously deranged." He leans into me to kiss me. "You come back here as soon as you leave the police station."

"I will, doll face," he says and pulls away as I watch him go.

Chapter Thirty

Gabe

Grabbing my phone out of my pocket, I call my father and tell him what happened and that I wouldn't be back to work today. I make it to the police station and check in with the front desk. I sit down, thinking about my house being burned fucking down.

"Mr. Walker," another detective calls for me, and I get up and walk to him. He takes me down a white hallway with rooms on both sides. He opens the door. "Please have a seat."

I pull out the chair and sit down. "Anything that I can do to help," I say, "but I have to say, I'm a little confused about all this."

"Well, hopefully I can shed some light on the situation with what she told us," he says, opening a file.

"So she said she started working for you three years ago. That it was platonic when your fiancée left. She said she thinks your fiancée left because she found out that you were in love with Ava."

"I was left at the altar. I have five hundred witnesses who can confirm I would have gotten married that day."

"She has text messages on her phone that she claims were sent from you."

I open my mouth. "Impossible because I never sent them."

"Well, I have the proof," he says, taking out her phone and putting it in front of me. I pick it up and am shocked that it's my fucking number and the texts are fucking making me blush. "Still sticking to your original statement, Mr. Walker?"

I snap my head up to look at him. "You're damn fucking straight." I take my phone out. "I have never ever texted any of my nurses, ever. Especially not of my dick."

"Are you having a child with one of your nurses?" he asks, leaning back.

I place my hands on the table. "This interview is over. I'm not going to answer any other questions without a lawyer present." I get up. "I'm telling you the truth. My tires have been slashed two times, two." I put my hands in my pocket. "And now my house has been burned down, and the person responsible for that is in another room somewhere." I look up at the ceiling. "Did she ever think that maybe someone was home when she decided to go all fatal attraction? Is anyone asking her what would have happened if anyone was home?"

"She wasn't thinking clearly," the detective says.

"Well, someone needs to make her start thinking clearly," I breathe out. "This is crazy, beyond crazy. I have never, ever, ever said or did anything that would have made her think I wanted her that way."

He doesn't say anything while he gets up and goes to the door. I walk out of the room the exact moment Ava is walking out of another room. She has black tear streaks down her cheeks. She runs to me, throwing her arms around my neck. "Oh, Gabe, you came for me," she cries. My hands take hold of her up arms and I push her away. She looks shocked by my actions. "I knew you would come."

"I didn't come for you. I would never come for you," I tell her, and she takes two steps back, her hand going to her chest. "You burned my house down." Anger now coming out of me. "What if Crystal was home and stuck inside? What if she or the baby were harmed?" The minute I mention the baby, she loses her mind.

"That bitch trapped you. How do you even know it's your baby?" she says. She lunges at me, stopped by the detective who was beside me. "It was supposed to be me. You were supposed to fall in love with me the minute Bethany left." She tries to worm her way out of the detective's arms. "For three years, I was your go-to, and then that bitch comes into the office, and all of a sudden, you don't care."

"I never ever looked at you any other way except professionally," I tell her.

"I know you love me. I see it every time you look over at me and smile. The way you always ask for me when there are all those other nurses."

"I think this has gone on long enough," the detective

says. "Mr. Walker, I will let you know if I need anything else."

I look at him and then at Ava, "Never. It was never going to happen." Then I walk out of the station. My head pounding so hard.

When I get back to Crystal's, I walk into the house and see her sleeping on the couch. Going to her, I squat down in front of her and kiss her lips. Her eyes open slowly, and she stretches out her arms. Pulling me close to her, she kisses my lips. "You're back."

"Yeah," I say while I rub her cheek with my thumb. "I just got back. The door wasn't locked."

"Well, considering the person after you burned your house down, I thought it was safe." She moves closer to my touch.

"For the time being, can we just lock it?" I stare at her. "How are you feeling?"

"Tired, hungry, happy, excited." She smiles. "Happy."

"I'm going to drive into town," I tell her. "I have to go and buy some stuff to wear."

"Oh, I want to come." She sits up, and I stand, holding my hand out to her. "Can we grab a cheeseburger? I'm dying for meat."

I raise my eyebrows at her. "Not that kind of meat." She kisses my chin. "Besides, according to the doctor, that meat is off limits."

"He never said anything about eating it?" I smack her ass while she walks in front of me. She grabs her purse and phone to text Hailey to tell her she is going into town.

"So tell me," she says while she buckles in, "what

happened at the police station?"

"Well," I say, driving out of town. "According to the police, I was in love with her, and that is the reason Bethany left town."

"Shut the fuck up," she says, and I laugh.

"Nope." I turn to look at her. "And she had texts that I apparently sent to her."

"She took your phone," she says to me, and I whip my head around to look at her. "Once, I saw her on your phone in the kitchen. She said you left it there by accident and she would return it."

"Motherfucker," I say. "I didn't even think of that. I usually just leave it in my office."

I see her shrugging her shoulders. "No clue, but she had it, and I remember because I noticed that ridiculous phone case."

"The periodic table isn't ridiculous," I tell her.

"Whatever. I saw her on it," she says. "So now what happens?"

"Tonight, I shop for new clothes, beg my girlfriend to sleep over at her house, and then tomorrow, I find two nurses."

"You never know. The doctor could say I can go back to work."

"We aren't risking anything. And by that, I mean"—I glare sideways at her—"you do fucking nothing."

"Wow," she pffts out, "with that attitude, you'd better call your mom and tell her to make up a bed since you're homeless."

I laugh at her. "Half of me is in you, which means

where you are, I am." I wink at her as she rolls her eyes. "Get used to it, doll face, because we have another five months. Then hopefully the rebuild will be ready just in time for the baby to be born and we can move in."

"Wow, you have all this mapped out?" she asks.

"Gotta say, doll face, best news I ever got was you carrying my baby." I pick up her hand, bringing it to my mouth. "So yeah, I have everything mapped out."

She doesn't answer me. Instead, she turns her head to look out the window, no doubt sending me to hell, but at least she's doing it with a smile.

Chapter Thirty-One

Crystal

I'm fucking waddling. Side to side like a penguin and I'm enjoying each and every single fucking second. My Crocs squeak while I walk to Gabe's office, my hand rubbing my stomach while our child kicks. I'm seven months pregnant today, seven months.

So much has changed in the past three months. Hailey moved out to go live with Walker, giving her share of the lease to Gabe, who weaseled his way in. The rebuild of the house that burned down is close to completion. Since the first visit with Dr. Sprung, it's been smooth sailing, so smooth he said I could work one day a week if I only do light paperwork. So, Gabe was overruled with his 'over my dead body' rule, and I work every Wednesday. All in all, he still gets under my skin, but I wouldn't want to be with anyone else.

I knock on the door before going in, seeing him sitting behind his desk. "Hey." I smile at him as he looks up and smiles when he sees me. I walk in and close the door while he walks around his desk. His baby blue dress shirt rolled up at the sleeves with the two buttons at the top opened. His khakis fitting him so perfectly.

Another thing that has been a go is sex. Thank fucking god, too, because with all these hormones, I'm surprised his dick isn't raw. I just can't get enough of him, but now with my belly, we've had to get creative, to say the least.

I waddle to him as he leans against his desk, his hands coming out to touch my stomach right away. "Hello, doll faces," he says, leaning in to kiss me and then leaning to kiss my belly. "Someone is active today," he says when our child kicks his hand.

"Yes." I nod. "That and I also just finished eating gummy bears."

He shakes his head, and I step in the middle of his outstretched legs, my hand going around his neck. "It's not my fault; it's the baby's."

He tries to wrap his hands around my waist but stops at my hips.

"I think I'm going to need a bigger size in scrubs," I say to him. The pants are fine since I tie them under my belly, but the shirt is almost like a tent and now is look-ing as if it's a crop top.

"Or you can stay home." He leans in, kissing my neck softly, then his tongue comes out, and I forget to tell him to fuck off. My hands on his chest start to open his but-tons on his shirt when a knock on the door stops me. "Come in," he says, his eyes twinkling.

I turn my head as soon as the door opens, and in steps

a woman who looks like she just stepped off the runway. Perfectly tailored clothes, her makeup flawless, her hair perfectly curled. One look and I know who this is—Bethany.

She looks at us in an embrace, and her face drops, turning white. I turn in his arms and my back to his chest as he places his hands on my stomach. "I …" She stops talking as soon as she notices my stomach.

"What are you doing here?" Gabe now stands up, moving me to the side where he holds my hand. "Who the fuck let you in?"

She stands there, her hands crossed in front of her. "I'm here to see your father, but he wasn't in his office, so …"

"So you decided it would be a good idea to come to mine?" he asks, his voice curt.

"I didn't know." She raises her hand to me. "I didn't know that."

"That I'm having a baby?" He smiles now, looking at me, his hands going around my shoulder, bringing me to him. "I am. Bethany, meet the love of my life. Well, the two loves of my life."

She blinks, not sure what to say, so Gabe continues. "Doll face, meet Bethany. Bethany, this is Crystal and Baby S." I got fed up with him calling the baby squirt, so he decided Baby S. it would be.

She nods at me, and I can see she's in shock as she tries to swallow. "It's nice to meet you."

I nod my head at her. It's not nice to meet me; it's the opposite of nice to meet me. "Well, I won't take any more of your time." She starts and turns around to leave.

"Wait," I say, and when she turns around, my hands now go around his waist. "Thank you."

"For what?" she asks, but she knows. A woman fucking knows.

"For leaving him at the altar. For throwing him away." I look up at him, into the eyes of the man I want to spend the rest of my life with, the man I want to wake up next to every morning. The man I want to hit with a broom sometimes, most times. "I have to believe we would have found each other anyway. In my heart, he was the missing piece, so thank you."

She doesn't say anything to me. She just nods her head and walks out. "Aww, with a speech like that, I'm going to think you like me."

I roll my eyes at him. "I had to say something. She was all there, perfect and skinny. With her tits perky praising god, and here I am with my gut hanging out, my boobs are all big and alien-like." I try to walk away from him, but he brings me closer to him.

"You love me," he teases me. Although I haven't come out and told him I love him yet. Well, at least not to his face. I tell him when he's asleep, and I watch him in a non-creepy stalker kind of way.

"I'm having your baby," I tell him. "I have to love you." I smile at him.

"Let's go. I have a surprise for you," he says, grabbing my hand as we walk out of the office. He holds my hand and puts me into the truck and helps me buckle in since I can't maneuver myself with a basketball in front of me.

"Where are we going?" I ask him.

"You'll see," he says, making his way to his house. Ava, is out on bail staying with her parents. Since it was her first offense it's most likely she won't get jail time, but we still have a restraining order against her. We haven't been there for over a month because the fumes wouldn't be good for me. I'm shocked when we pull up, and I see that it's finished.

"Oh my god, it's done," I say, unbuckling myself and pushing myself out.

"It is." He grabs my hand as we walk in. "There isn't any furniture yet," he says, walking upstairs to the bedrooms. "Well, one room is done," he says, walking to the bedroom with double doors. He releases my hand to push open the two doors, and I gasp out in shock.

"What?" I walk in, taking in the prettiest nursery I have ever seen. It looks like a picture from a magazine. The walls are painted gray, one wall with white circles on them. A white crib sits against the wall with gray and white bedding. Frames of animals hang all around the room. "You said you wanted animals." I turn to him as I take in the little sheep rocking chair for the baby in the corner. The white dresser and white changing table. The closet opened to show me baby pajamas hanging, waiting to be worn. I look around and then see a rocking chair with a side table. A picture of the two of us beside it. I walk into the middle of the room, taking it all in. The bunnies on the shelf, the diapers on the table, the blankets all washed and folded. "It was a gift from my parents."

"What?" I turn to look at him. "This is too much."

"You have no idea. If it was up to my parents, they would have had the animals brought in and living in the backyard to make you happy." His parents have hands down accepted me with open arms.

It's so perfect. I go to the crib, looking inside, and I turn and see him in the middle of the room on bended knee. "What?" I whisper, my hands flying to my mouth.

"I had this whole speech prepared on how to ask you to marry me in bullet form because I knew you would argue with me about it." I am crying out a sob and a laugh. "Last year, I thought there was no way I would survive being crushed. There was no way I would ever be able to go on. But then one day, I got up and knew it would be okay, and then I met you. That exact night you fell into my lap." I walk to him, my hands going to his face. "My father told me that if I loved Bethany, I would have gone after her. I thought he was just feeding me bullshit, but …" He looks down and then up with a tear in his eye. "If you ever left me, I would turn over every fucking stone there was to find you because I know I can't live without you."

I lean down to kiss his lips. "Can I say yes now?"

"I'm not done," he says, smiling as my thumbs rub his face. "I want to wake up every single day to you; I want to come home to you. I want to fight with you and then make up with you; I want to live the rest of my life with you by my side."

"I love you," I finally say out loud, and he smiles so

big his eyes crinkle at the corner. "I tell you that when you're sleeping every single night."

"I know," he whispers, "I hear it."

"Now can I say yes?" I ask him with tears streaming down our cheeks.

"Will you marry me?" he asks me, but I'm already nodding my head.

"Yes, I'll marry you and carry however many children God decides to give us. I'll love you with every single thing that I have even when I want to throw something at you."

He opens the ring case, showing me a beautiful rose gold square diamond with white diamonds in the band. He slips the ring on my finger as I laugh and cry, bending to kiss him.

I don't say anything as he gets up and kisses me again, and this time, my mind wanders back to the dreams that have haunted me. My baby girl who looks like her father but had my eyes. Unexpected, this whole thing must be my unexpected love story.

Epilogue One
Crystal

"I think this might be it," I say, getting up in the middle of the night two months after we moved in. I'm officially three days past my due date and impatient to meet my little one.

"That's what you've said for the past week," Gabe says quietly from beside me. He turns over. "It's three a.m."

"I know, but it feels different." I look at him as I roll out of bed. "We should have sex again to get things going."

"No," he says loudly, "I'm pretty sure I have no sperm left." I laugh at him. He might be right, though. We had sex five times today, twice before he left for work, twice when he got home, and once before we went to bed, three yesterday, and three the day before.

"No, Gabe," I huff out, going to the bathroom, "I'm telling you, I feel it in my back," I say and then pain rips through me, causing me to double over and scream.

Gabe flies out of bed to me. "Breathe," he says as I glare up at him. "Shit, this is it."

"I told you it was different," I hiss, panting. "I have to take a shower. Help me."

"You can't take a shower. You're having contractions. We have to get to the hospital," he tells me.

"But we had sex," I say right before another sharp pain hits me, and I pant through it with him counting. "I'm full of your sperm."

"Doll face," he says, "with the stuff that is going to be coming out of you, the least of your worries should be the sperm." I glare at him. "Now if you don't get your ass in the fucking truck, I'm going to call Nanny and Gram."

I gasp. Nanny and my mom came to town two days ago and are staying with Gram till the baby is born, and then they will come and help us. "You wouldn't dare." My stomach tenses as another contraction bears down on me and tears form in my eyes. "Oh my god."

"Sit down on the bed. I need to start timing the contractions." He runs to pull on his pants and a t-shirt while grabbing me a dress because nothing fucking fits me. "Where the fuck are the keys?" He runs around searching for the keys that are in his hand. When I moan as another one comes, I ask, "Can we go please?" He holds my hand, walking down the stairs with me, helping me in the car and buckling me in. The pain is okay for now, but the minute he starts driving, it gets so much worse.

"Holy shit, this hurts," I say as another one hits me.

"Fuck, they are like three minutes apart," he says and

starts speeding. "Breathe."

"What the fuck does it look like I'm do—" I stop and then look down as water fills the front seat. I look up at him. "My water just broke," I say as the pain rips through me.

"We are there in three minutes," he says, the twenty-five-minute ride taking only seventeen minutes. He pulls up to the emergency room door. Parking the truck, he rushes around while another contraction hits. This time, it causes me to scream as I hold the dashboard. He comes running with a wheelchair and a nurse. "I'm here," he says, panting. I look at him and see that my calm, cool man is the opposite of calm and cool. His face is now pale, and his eyes wild. "Are you okay?" he asks while I get out of the truck and into the chair.

"Sir, you can't leave your vehicle here," the nurse yells after him.

"I got it." I hear Walker yell from behind us, seeing Hailey run to my side.

"I'm here," she says as I burst out crying. "It's going to be okay," she whispers to me.

"I'm so scared," I whisper back to her. "If anything happens to me ..."

"Not this again," she starts. "No more fucking emergency birthing videos for you." She presses the button for the elevator, looking at Gabe. "Why the fuck did you bring them home?"

"Me?" he says. "She took them from the fucking office." I did. I think back to when he came home and saw me in a puddle of tears in the middle of the living room crying because I knew there was no way to go through that pain without dying.

"Holy shit," I hiss, my stomach getting so tight I swear it's going to pop. "Aaahhhhhh."

"Fuck." I hear Gabe say, the doors opening and a nurse meeting us there.

"You must be the Walkers. I'm Jackie, and I'm going to be with you guys tonight."

"It's like she's our waitress," I whisper to Hailey who just smiles.

"Now, follow me." She smiles at me. "And let's get you hooked up to a monitor." They wheel me into a room where Hailey helps me take off my dress and then gasps at the veins in my boobs as I get into a hospital gown.

"It's like I'm a weird experiment gone wrong," I tell her. "It's like neon blue."

"You're beautiful," she says as I groan out with another contraction. When the nurse starts hooking me up to the machine, the sound of the baby's heartbeat fills the room.

"So this machine is going to monitor the heart rate, and then over here"—she points at the other part of the machine—"that measures your contractions." And right then, a contraction starts.

"Breathe," Gabe says from the other side of me, watching the monitor the whole time.

"Really?" I say between clenched teeth. "Thank god, you're here to tell me that I need to breathe while a human is trying to tear through me."

"Okay," he says while the nurse tells me to spread

my legs so she can check me. "Looks like you're seven centimeters."

"I want drugs," I say, right before I close my legs and start the heee, heee, hooo, hooo.

"I'm afraid it's too late for that," Jackie tells me.

"No," I say, looking at her and then Gabe. "Override her. You're a doctor, and she's a nurse. Tell her she's wrong."

"Doll face." He leans down kissing me.

"No," I say, shaking my head, the tears coming now. "No, no, no, I can't do this without drugs."

"Yes, you can," he tells me. "You're the strongest person I know."

For the next hour, the contractions come fast and hard, so hard, I'm crying out in pain. Gabe looks like he's about to throw a shit fit with the nurse. "Time to see what's going on down there," Jackie says. "Perfect," she says, getting up and going to the phone. "Dr. Sprung, it's time," she says, and then springs into action, turning the light on in the crib. She unfolds the blankets as Dr. Sprung comes in.

"I heard someone is ready to meet their parents?" he says all chipper and shit, and I swear I want to kick him in the balls.

"I need drugs," I say, panting, the sweat dripping from my forehead. I'm so tired. I'm so, so tired; it feels like I just ran a fucking marathon without resting.

"Doll face," Gabe says, grabbing my hand while Jackie puts my feet up in the stirrups. "We are going to meet our baby."

Dr. Sprung puts on his gloves, sitting on the stool, and scoots over to me. "I can see the baby's head, so when you have your next contraction, I need you to bear down and push," he says, looking at the monitor. "Another one is coming so get ready. And push."

Gabe, Jackie, and Hailey all count to ten while I bear down and push with everything I have. "Okay, now breathe. That was good," he says, and for the next forty-five minutes, I push and push and push.

"It's too much," I cry, my body limp. "I can't do it anymore," I say, my eyes closing. "I just ... it hurts so much," I sob.

"The baby's heart rate is dropping," Jackie says, and my eyes spring open. "Dr. Sprung."

Gabe bends down next to me, pushing my sweaty hair away from my face and looking in my eyes. "Doll face, I know you're tired," he says, his thumb catching the tear running down my face. "You've done so good." He kisses my nose. "So fucking good, but you need to try one more time."

I sob. "I can't. I just can't."

I don't hear what is going on around me until I hear Dr. Sprung. "We need to get the baby out." He looks at me. "Crystal, it's important we get the baby out."

"Gabe." I look at him.

"You can do this. You are so strong."

"Push," Dr. Sprung says. "Keep pushing, keep pushing," he says, and I push with everything I have left. "Okay, stop pushing, the head is out," he says while Gabe looks down and tears are flowing down his face.

"Okay, one more big push. Go, go, go, go."

I push so hard, I yell out while I push and then the most beautiful thing in the world is happening when the doctor places my baby on my chest and the tears rip through me. "Oh my god, my baby," I say, grabbing the baby on my chest. Gabe's hands cover mine, and the only thing I can say is, "My baby." I laugh and cry all at the same time, the baby's wails filling the room.

"Congratulations, you have a daughter," Dr. Sprung says, and just like that, my dreams come true. The dreams that haunted me ever since I got here have come true.

I look up at Gabe, who kisses me. "I love you."

"We have a daughter." I look at Hailey who has her hand over her mouth and cries softly. "I have a daughter." Words that I never thought I would say.

I look down at my daughter, her eyes blinking while she quietly looks around. "Hey, beautiful, it's me, Mommy," I say, smiling. The tiredness gone, the pain all worth this moment right here. With my daughter lying on my chest, and the man who I would move mountains for by my side, I have my love story. This is my love story. It may not be conventional, it may not be the way I would have planned it, but it is the right one for me.

We met unexpectedly, the universe already aligning our stars, and no matter what we did, it was always going to be us. No matter what we did, it was always our unexpected that turned into love.

Epilogue Two
Gabe

Four Years Later . . .

"Daddy, Daddy, look, a seashell," Savannah yells, running to pick up the shell she just spotted. Her blond curls blow in the wind when she finds it and turns to wave at her mother who sits with her coffee in her hand. We are taking our daily walk on the beach while Crystal sits on the sand, watching us. She never did come back to work. Nope, not my wife. She stayed home and made every single moment count. I don't even think that Savannah has cried more than ten tears since she was born. Thinking about it makes me smile.

"Make sure you don't get your feet wet," I tell her when she places the seashell in my hand.

"I won't, Daddy," she says, running off when I look back and seeing Crystal now smiling at us as she leans her arms back, her big pregnant stomach showing. We are having another miracle baby in a month, a boy this time, and I can't fucking wait.

Best thing to happen to me was meeting Crystal and having my daughter, but I have to say the best day of my life, was when I stood at that altar and watched her walk down the aisle to me. Her eyes brimming with tears as I held our daughter in my arms. We vowed to love each other in good times and bad times, and she vowed not to kill me. When I slipped that wedding band on her finger, my life just felt so fucking complete, I can't explain it. It was a sense of peace, a sense of belonging, a sense that the world was right.

"Daddy," Savannah says, coming back to me, "can we go walk?" She puts her small hand in mine while the other small hand tries to push the hair away from her face. "Not a long walk," she says, looking up at me and smiling.

"Only for a little walk. Okay." I lean down and kiss her nose. "We don't want to leave Mommy too long, okay?" I tell her as she nods her head. "Wave at Mommy," I tell her as she turns around and waves at Crystal, who's watching our every move. We turn and start walking down the beach, and it's at that exact moment I stop and think back to that day I had this vivid dream of walking on the beach with a little girl looking back at someone sitting watching us. All along, it was there; all along, she was the woman in my dreams. "Let's go, doll face," I tell her as she shakes her head.

"I'm not doll face. Mommy is doll face," she says while we walk down the beach. "I'm angel face."

So, on that warm sunny day on that beach, two dreams came together unexpectedly!

The End of my unexpected love story, or just the beginning!

Stay tuned for Samantha and Blake's Story

Broken Love Story

Samantha:

I had the perfect life; a husband who loved me, and two kids who were my world.

Until someone else answered his phone and my perfect life shattered.

When he died, I was left with answers he couldn't give me and a box full of lies.

He left me broken.

Blake:

I fell in love when I was fifteen, knowing she was the one.

For five years, she was my everything—my every breath, every heartbeat, every thought.

She made me promise to move on, promise to find love again, but I broke those promises because I can't move on.

Two broken souls brought together by tragedy and heartbreak.

Can a broken love story be fixed?

Books By Natasha Madison

Something Series
Something So Right
Something So Perfect
Something So Irresistible

Tempt Series
Tempt The Boss
Tempt The Playboy
Tempt The Neighbor–2018

Heaven & Hell Series
Hell and Back
Pieces of Heaven

True Love Series
Pefrect Love Story
Unexpected Love Story
Broken Love Story

Novellas
Cheeky
Until Brandon (Kindle World)
Madison Rose Books
Only His

Acknowledgments

Every single time I keep thinking it's going to be easy. It takes a village to help and I don't want to leave anyone out.

My Husband: I love you, I don't tell you enough. Thank you for letting me sit in bed most of the day writing, and for not busting my chops when I don't cook. Oh wait you do!

My Kids: Matteo, Michael, and Erica, Thank you for letting me do this. Thank you for being proud of me, I love you honey bunches and oats!

Crystal: My hooker and bestie. What don't you do for me? Everyone needs someone like you in their corner and I am so blessed than you chose to be in mine. I can't begin to thank you for the support, love and encouragement along the way.

Rachel: You are my blurb bitch. Each time you do it without even reading this book and you rocked it. I'm so happy that I ddin't give up when you ignored my many messages.

Meghan: I'm so so proud to call you my friend. Thank you for making me make that list, and making me see I can actually achieve it.

Jamie & Sarah: Thank you for being in my corner, and always having my back.

Lori: I don't know what I would do without you in my life. You take over and I don't even have to ask or worry because I know everything will be fine, because you're a rock star, I'm also scared of that whip!

Denise: The hole finder. I can't put into word how honored I am that you took Max and made me make him even more Epic! I can't wait to bring Denise to life!

Melissa: My cover girl, I have more covers than stories, but I know you won't let me stop. Thank you for sending me covers while I sleep so I don't yell at you before you go to bed. I love you.

Beta girls: Teressa, Natasha M, Lori, Sandy, Yolanda, and Carmen, Yamina. For three weeks I bombarded your messages with chapters and you ate it up. Thank you for holding my hand, telling me when things sucked and for being by my side.

Madison Maniacs: This little group went from two people to so much more and I can't thank you guys enough. This group is my go to, my safe place. You push me and get excited for me and I can't wait to watch us grow even bigger!

Mia: I'm so happy that Nanny threw out Archer's Voice and I needed to tell you because that snowballed to a friendship that is without a doubt the best ever!

Neda: You answer my question no matter how stupid they sound. Thank you for being you, thank you for everything!

Julie: Thank you for taking my book with all it's mistakes and making it pretty, or as pretty as it can be.

BLOGGERS. THANK YOU FOR TAKING A CHANCE ON ME. You give so much of yourself effortlessly and you are the voice that we can't do this without.

Made in the USA
Monee, IL
21 June 2023

36473630R00152